The Iron Ore Miner's Son

Published in association with
EVC Group, 4022 Oakridge, Houston, Texas 77009

ISBN: 0-9661137-0-5

Printed in USA.
Book design by Jeff DeBevec

*Dedicated to the memory of
my father and mother,
Anton and Agnes DeBevec*

Acknowledgements

Dad has always been proud of his roots. Stories of his youth were a cherished delight for Mike and me as kids and we reveled in their telling. This memoir saves the stories to be told again, along with the experiences, philosophies, and anecdotes that are the family treasure and a gift to the reader.

Anyone who has written a book knows that the author is just one of several people on the team. When Dad informed us that he was writing "the book," I really didn't give much thought at the time to the challenge that lay ahead. As designated editor/publisher and family member, I was bent on contributing to the fullest. Along the way however, I discovered that the book was, to borrow a phrase, not something I should try at home. The kindness and talents of several people were brought together to bring *The Iron Ore Miner's Son* to life.

Thanks to Elisabeth Lindheim who cheerfully took on the daunting task of converting a thousand pages of handwritten manuscript to computer files that could be edited; to Polly Robertus who took a rough edit and corrected grammar, organized chapters, and edited every line into the polished book you have in your hands; to Diane McHale for proof-reading the final manuscript; and to Karen Malnar whose handsome jacket design has given us such a respectable look.

I also want to express gratitude to many friends and family members for their ideas and encouragement along the way, especially to Frank and Lois Smith, Martha Thomas, Joel Barna Laura Furman, Gary Easterly, and my brother Mike — and to Mum for being there.

Jeff DeBevec
September 1997

Introduction

THIS BOOK IS NOT FICTION. All names and places and events are actual. There may be some hyperbole; I use it to emphasize and illustrate, not deceive.

All my writings originated in daily notes I scribbled on any available paper: toilet paper, old envelopes, gum wrappers, magazines and newspapers, grocery sacks, napkins, receipts, credit cards, ID cards, or business cards.

Some of my best thoughts come at night when the genesis of an idea forces me out of bed. I stagger blindly to the dark kitchen where I have a permanent note pad and a jar of pencils. I scratch out a word or two, never more, grope my way back to bed, and immediately fall asleep. In the morning, I expand the note and in time a story is born.

I have always felt that, whatever our role in the drama of life, we have to do "our thing." Our deeds, behavior, prayers, and love toward one another are woven together into the whole scheme of existence. The deeper we realize our spiritual unity with life, and with each other, and especially with our God, the more we can share in the miracles and wonders of life.

In retrospect, my life has been a vital, radiating one with an abundance of energy, joy, optimism, and enthusiasm in most of the things I attempted. I can assure you I was not ready to hide my light under a bushel. I was never given any material wealth by anybody, but somebody surely gave me a plethora of talents. I always tried to be a source of reinforcing cheerfulness to everyone around me. I felt that life must have meaning far beyond anything I could comprehend. I am not being hyperbolic when I state that I was always a "happy-to-get-up-in-the-morning" guy. I knew that I had only the present in which to live, so I must glean as much good as possible out of it. I'm sure I didn't always have a gentle word for everyone. But I had enough for most and I did offer simple acts of kindness and charity that brought me intense pleasure and far-reaching results. I loved to live each day as if I were to die by the morrow, so I always lived fully, right where I was.

I am now in my senior years and, as I reflect upon my life, I see good unfolding in all my experiences. No matter how unpleasant life sometimes outwardly appeared, I am convinced that I was always held securely in the hand of God.

I am deeply indebted to the following people. Without them this book would never have come to fruition. They are loved ones who encouraged, critiqued, and corrected what I wrote.

First, my Canadian wife, Olive (Annie), who was coerced into listening to every original page for hundreds of hours over five years and who helped me correct errors, suggested changes, and proofread every one of the 1,000 original pages. Second, my confidante and great friend Frank A. "Mr. Canada" Smith, a retired advertising executive for the Toronto Star, for taking the time from his many projects to review my writings. And finally, our son Jeff, my editor and publisher, for his efforts and patience in dealing with constant requests for changes to the manuscript.

I dedicate this book to my dad, Anton, the iron ore miner

who left Slovenia in the Austro-Hungarian empire in 1903, alone, young, penniless, and unable to speak a word of English. He carried all his worldly possessions in a wicker basket to seek his fortune in the U.S., to mine the bowels of Minnesota's iron range.

I also dedicate this to my mother, Agnes, who joined him a year later as his sixteen-year-old bride, and to their union, which produced one daughter and six sons, including the sixth, Joseph, the peripatetic author of this book.

And I dedicate it to the memory of my departed first wife Dorothy, mother of our sons, Jeff and Mike, and to the second family I gained with my marriage to Olive Gill in 1984: my daughters Carol and Elaine and son John, who have so genuinely welcomed me into their own families.

What a group! I am so proud of all of them. Without them I would never have had such a challenging, interesting, exciting, and rewarding life. I am eternally grateful to you and to all the wonderful people, too numerous to mention, who influenced my life and challenged me to do better.

Joseph J. DeBevec

Table of Contents

Immigrants

WHEN MY DAD ANTON LEFT AUSTRIA in 1903, he, like so many immigrants, had heard that America had "silver dripping from the trees and streets paved with gold." He believed a promise from some iron ore mine owners that he could enjoy a life of luxury here. Of course that was pure propaganda. The United States could not muster enough workers from the white Anglo-Saxon Protestant majority who were the country's ruling class in the late 19th and early 20th centuries. They had to inveigle and encourage massive hordes of immigrants from Europe. That siren enticed many strong, young, uneducated men from Europe. They would build this country on the strength of their backs. America as we know it today would never have existed without the dedication of hundreds of thousands of immigrants who flooded our country, believing promises and visions of prosperity. To these hapless dreamers fell the dirty work, the low pay, and the long hours.

At times we were subjected to rudeness, ridicule, or denigration for being poor immigrants. Although this made a difficult life more difficult for immigrants, most of us had the intestinal fortitude to rise above it (or sometimes fight it!). We were all raised by strong European families. Although I was born to a family of poor, badly educated Austrian peasants, we benefited from their strong religious background, law-abiding moral codes, strict rules, work ethic, and respect for authority. It gave our family the strength and guidance we needed through many of life's difficult times.

Miner's Life

In the early 1900's, the life of a miner was really tough. My dad, and later my five brothers, worked in the "Hole" for the Oliver Iron Ore Mining Company. The miners would pick up their carbide lamps, attach the lamps to their helmets, get into "the cage" (elevator) and descend into the bowels of the earth. The cage went as low as 1400 feet deep to discharge these poor immigrants. I heard that at one time, the miners had to take canaries in cages with them; if the bird died, the miner would know the tunnels were filling with gas and might have time to run to the cage hole, ring the bell, and hope the elevator would stop at his floor.

Besides poor pay, miners endured many accidents. Anyone who got hurt too badly to work didn't get paid. Even if they weren't injured, they'd be pain-wracked after an eight-to-ten hour shift. They were often sick with colds, coughs, and consumption (the dreaded miner's disease), caused by water constantly dripping on them.

My dad worked hard for a year, and saved his hard-earned dollars. His pay was about $3 a day. He had left his young girl-friend, Agnes, behind and had promised her that, when he made enough money, he would send for her. Finally, after what seemed an eternity, she joined him.

Anton DeBevec and Agnes Petrich were married by Father Bilban at Holy Family Church in Eveleth, Minnesota. In those days, Father Bilban had to crowd many marriage masses into one day to accommodate the tremendous influx of young European girlfriends arriving to join their miner boyfriends. Years later, a friend of my father's, Martin Shukle, Sr. told me that he and his newly married bride were leaving down the aisle of the church as my dad and his beloved Agnes passed them on the way to the altar.

Tarpaper Shack

Our home of rough lumber and a dirt floor was part of a cluster of similar shacks built by my dad and other miners on land they did not own. They so congested the land that many times no more than a foot separated the shacks. Our one-story, three-section shack stood at the edge of the Adams Iron Ore Mining Company's open-pit mine, a yawning hole where the miners dug with pick and shovel. All of the miners wanted to be as close as possible to the pit or to the underground mine for an easy walk home after their miserable, ten-hour shifts. It was not until many years later that small buses hauled the miners to their designated mines. (These buses were the beginning of today's present Greyhound bus chain, started by the Fitzgerald Brothers in Eveleth.)

My dad, Anton DeBevec, like the rest of the miners, built his own shack from rough two-by-fours and eight-inch planks hewn from logs by a crude, single-blade saw. The planks were never kiln-dried then, so they warped, which caused considerable problems in construction and warding off the cold. Often the shacks were patched and supported with parts of dynamite boxes the miners broke apart and hauled home. The boxes made good kindling too!

The shacks had flat roofs. They were covered with tar paper to ward off the freezing weather and the wind-blown dust from the ore dumps. My parents' shack was a poor haven for the

eventual arrival of seven children — generally in frustrating, ago-
nizing, and unhealthy circumstances.

But this was my dad's castle, home to the loves and lives
of a poor young miner and his bride, thousands of miles from their
homeland in Europe, with few relatives or friends, speaking
almost no English. From this dilapidated shack sprang the parade
of DeBevec progeny, beginning with my saintly sister Aggie, born
in 1905. Tony followed in 1906. Johnny came in 1908, Rudy in
1910, Frankie in 1912. I, Joey came along in 1915, followed by
Louis, the final son, in 1917. All of us were born without a doctor.
Women helped delivered their neighbors' children in those days.

By 1906, after her first two children were born, my poor
mother had figured out that those tales of gold and silver lining the
streets were false propaganda. She was a smart little cookie, and
she knew Dad's income as a miner was not sufficient to care for
their growing family. So they scrounged up some more unfinished
lumber and built two small additions to their original one-room
shack, each about the size of modern bathrooms. Into these rooms
my mother installed boarders: young, single men newly arrived
from Europe to be miners. These strong, husky Europeans found
jobs easy to come by; what they needed was someone to provide
them a bed, fix their lunch buckets, wash their clothes, iron their
one shirt for Sunday mass, and be a mother-like figure and confidante. My mother charged a small monthly fee for all these services.

The mines had three shifts of eight hours each. Mother was
smart. She rented one room to three different young men. Each
was on a different shift, so she could sell the bed three times in one
day. As each worker got up to release the bed to the next, Mother
gave him his meal, prepared his lunch bucket — and off he went.

Mother also did their laundry. This was no easy feat in the
winter when she had to hang the long, woolen underwear on our

clothesline in freezing weather. The underwear would freeze stiff, hanging from the clotheslines like effigies. Mother would then have to gather them — arms and legs sticking out every which way — and bring them into the shack to thaw.

Her lot was hard, but my mother used to say, "No matter how poor we are, we have to keep our home clean because we never know when Christ will come to our door."

Living as we did was not pleasant. The huge smoke-belching steam engine that hauled ore cars on tracks within just a few feet of the shack compounded the unpleasantness. The constant screeching of the wheels, the black smoke permeating the shack, and the jarring rumble were not conducive to restful sleep. We did, however, enjoy a blessing in the midst of these pathetic conditions. The steam engine burned coal, and the man who stoked its furnace was compassionate toward the poor miners. He routinely emptied a couple of shovelsful of coal into Dad's yard as the train passed. This was truly a bonanza, because Dad could not afford a bushel basket of coal. I doubt the mine owners were ever aware of these acts of mercy as they slept in their warm, flannel sheets in cozy, heated mansions.

Homesick

By 1911, Dad had been slaving for eight years, hauling "red gold" out of the dark, deep caves of Mother Earth. Illuminated only by carbide lamps attached to his helmet, he had endured eight years of backbreaking labor, drenched in sweat and the cold, dark water of underground seeps.

It was Mother, however, who wanted to leave that horizon of red-drenched snow covering ugly mountains of discarded dirt. She wanted to go home to Austria, with its edelweiss, snow-capped, green-forested mountains, crisp air, luscious farmland, gardens full of vegetables, and the comforting silence of a small village.

Dad felt he had everything he needed around him, and couldn't understand why she would want to leave. I don't know how long the discussion about leaving the United States lasted. I can only tell you that Mother won.

Sometime in 1911, they packed up their meager belongings in roped paper boxes and gathered their brood of children, none over the age of six. They abandoned the shack to whomever wanted it and left for Austria. Mother was pregnant with Frankie at the time.

It will always be a mystery to me how they managed the 5,000-mile trek back to their homeland with scant knowledge of English, meager funds, and no knowledge of transportation schedules. Nevertheless, somehow they completed the journey, which necessitated buses and trains across the U.S., an Atlantic crossing, and a traversal of Europe to the land of their births. Their miraculous sojourn was blessed with an absolute faith in a protective God.

After weeks of what was probably complete confusion, they finally arrived in Grohovo Pre Cerknica (Grove near the town of Cerknica), their birthplace in Slovenia. At first, they lived with relatives and charitable neighbors, but they soon began building a new home. After his eight years as a miner in the U.S., Dad was hardly rich, but he must have saved enough to start the structure. He hired Italian artisans from Trieste to help him. It was a large home, compared with the tarpaper shack, with a connecting balcony over stables for the horses and cattle, a barn, and granary. The balcony had hand-carved wooden trellis-like supports. Near the apex of the roof, a square granite stone carried two initials A.D. (Anton DeBevec).

My brother Frankie was born there in September 1912.

Life was certainly a change from the shack community in northern Minnesota, but the family continued to live frugally, raising crops, cattle, and pigs. The pleasant climate and ambiance of the Austrian countryside compensated for the daily labor in the fields. They lived in this idyllic place for about two years.

Then it seems, just as suddenly as their decision to return to their homeland, the yearning to be back in America, the land of the free, beckoned them to return to the U.S.A.

Back to the U.S.A.

They sold all their personal possessions, including the livestock. Government regulations prohibited them from selling the land and the house. So they gave the house to Mother's youngest brother, John Petrich. He and his wife were still living there on my visit to Yugoslavia in 1975.

In October 1913, they packed up their meager possessions (they were always meager) in boxes and began their long trek back to Minnesota with four of the children. Rudy, age three, remained in Austria with our grandparents. My grandfather and grandmother, whom I never met, had no children left to comfort and assist them. They asked my mother and dad to give them one of their children to ease the pain of our parent's absence. My dad agreed without hesitation. This may seem terribly sacrificial to you, but not to East Europeans.

On their trip back to Minnesota, the family traveled the absolutely cheapest way possible. As their ship crossed the Atlantic, the weather was horrendous and all the immigrants were packed in the bottom of the ship with the rats. It wasn't first class, it was "no" class.

The stench of so many people living in such close quarters for so long was horrible. They had little privacy. Buckets served as toilets. The crowding in the cold North Atlantic weather created a perfect, cruel environment for disease. A wave of deadly diphtheria ran rampant, and poor baby Frank got it. It was very serious. The ship's poor doctor kept an endless pace, going from one afflicted person to another with the most meager of medicinal supplies.

To prevent the whole ship from becoming infected, he had to order passengers in the worst state, whom he considered incurable, to be thrown overboard. Late one night, the doctor gave Mother the ultimatum: Frankie was to be slid into the sea. Mother pleaded with him for a little time. He relented, but gave her only until early morning when he would return to check on the baby. Mother gathered Dad and the other children around her and the baby. They prayed the rosary for what seemed hours, begging for a miracle to prevent Frankie's being lowered into the icy North Atlantic. Around four in the morning, the crisis passed and his fever made a dramatic slide downward. The doctor returned as promised, noted his recovery and spared the infant from a watery grave.

Eight years later, at age eleven, our grandparents finally "released" Rudy. He made the long journey back to rejoin our family in Minnesota, traveling alone with a small, wicker valise that held all his worldly possessions. He spoke no English and had no food with him. He had very little money. But he made the 5,000-mile trek to meet his parents, sister and five brothers, none of whom he could recognize. The family was whole again, back in the U.S.A.

Life on "Da Range"

"A miner is like a duck, it can run a little bit,
swim a little bit, and fly a little bit, but nothing perfect."

Early Life

I ARRIVED IN A TARPAPER SHACK March 11, 1915, a bitterly cold, windswept day in Eveleth, Minnesota.

My only sister, Aggie, the eldest child in the family and truly my second mother, has told me about our early lives under those poor circumstances. Heat was a luxury we could not afford, which made dirt and rough-hewn floors even more uncomfortable. Food was sometimes difficult to find. According to Aggie, the mines had been on strike for three months before my birth. With no income, we could afford no food. There were no strike benefits. Terrible tensions festered between miners, friends, neighbors, and even relatives. Few dared to "break the line," but Aggie recalls that Dad did. He had to, with six starving kids.

Fortunately my mother's sister, Frances, and her husband Gregor, fresh from their homeland, arrived when Mother and I so desperately needed their help. They were rich, in our estimation. They did not have children, so they did not have to support anyone but themselves. And, oh, what beautiful people! In their short time with us (they soon moved to Chicago), they were a constant inspiration with their charity, and solicitude for us all. Aggie told me that, on the day of my birth, "Teta," as we affectionately called our Aunt Frances, brought in what Aggie called an "emaciated chicken" for soup. Owing to Teta and that soup, my mother had enough nourishment to develop some milk for her newest child — me!

We never got birth certificates. For all the government knew, none of us existed. Many years later, in 1955, I wanted to take my first cruise and I needed a passport. A year of intensive research revealed that there was no record of any of my family being born. We were all baptized in the Holy Family Catholic Church and our births were recorded there. However, the United States government will not accept church records for passport applications. After months of frustrating inquiries, calls, and letters, I got my first passport on the strength of my eldest brother Tony's testimony that he was nine years old at my birth and had witnessed it!

First Home

Around 1920 Dad bought a small lot at 706 Summit Street, near Pugel's Hill and the cow pasture, a new "suburban development" at the extreme east end of town. Having finally secured his first piece of territory, he had no money left over to erect a home. So he moved his tumbledown mining shack to his precious new lot. He somehow found enough rough lumber to build a pig barn at the rear of the lot, and suddenly our social status increased with our own pigs to feed, fatten, and slaughter. Dad built a small smokehouse to cure all those precious pig parts and smoke his own sausage. Now we were truly living high on the hog!

Knowing Mother, she kept after Dad, sternly reminding him that our move from Old Town to this admirable hillside lot had changed nothing. We were still in a shack sleeping three or four to a bed. The only thing we had gained was the loss of the rumbling, belching train.

The shack we moved from Old Town was now in the middle of the lot where Dad was going to build our new mansion. Mother was the brains in our family. Her solution to this problem was to tear down the shack, save the lumber, slaughter the pigs, clean out the pig barn, and move the family into the pig barn until the new house was at least roofed, framed, and floored. And that is what we did.

One of my first recollections was living in the pig barn. I remember not minding the slaughter of the pigs because one of those ungrateful hogs had destroyed one of my proudest possessions — a cute straw sailor hat (used) that a benevolent neighbor had given me. I loved hats — any kind — and still do to this day, especially on women.

The lots where we were building were only 25' x 100', which forced the homes to be narrow and tall. Every lot owner used as much land as he possibly could so the homes were only two or three feet apart. I remember cogitating on a toilet seat in our bathroom upstairs and hearing with clarity the loud "whoosh" of the neighbor's toilet being flushed a few feet away.

Everyone helped build each others' homes then; family members, relatives, and neighbors swarmed like ants all over the house. They built it with a lot of unpaid help — no plans, no advisers, no salaries, no unions, no strikes, no blueprints, no wage negotiations. Mother was the official unpaid architect. She designed it daily: "I want this here and this there." My mother's first order was for a full basement — of solid split rock. No poured cement! Rock was cheap, as the hills near Eveleth were full of it. My dad and his neighbors and sons split boulders by hand with chisels and sledge hammers, blasting the big ones with dynamite that Dad finagled from his mining friends. They hauled each heavy piece of split rock by wheelbarrow. Mother watched daily with an eagle eye to make sure every rock was well-mortised before it was mortared. Dad could do anything in manual labor or construction, but his mortaring and fitting of split stones were masterful. In a very short time the house rose from its foundation: the wooden studs, the beams, the rough floors, the peaked roof braces, and the roof covered with planks. A huge two-story house! To us, the skeleton wooden frame reached out to God.

When they drove the final nail into the last plank of the roof, all the workers yelled lustily as they hauled and nailed a freshly cut spruce tree to the apex of the roof. This "topping" tradition was a symbolic ritual to thank God for all His help through all these workers.

Every worker's home in the area was built in such a manner. All the male neighbors came pouring in to help, and all the women and girls came to cook for the ravenous laborers. All experts! Everyone helping each other. I mourn the passing of this kind of altruistic, compassionate, charitable neighborhood culture. How could we have lost it? I pray we find it again.

Life on Summit Street

We kids had many duties to help our parents. Our chores included picking up slop for the hogs from neighbors, slopping the hogs, cutting, splitting, and stacking wood for the kitchen stove and furnace, shoveling snow from the sidewalks, cleaning the pig pens, scrubbing floors, stomping grapes in barrels with woolen socks on our feet to make wine, helping to repair the house, painting, hauling groceries, and paying bills.

We also had the continual arduous labor of planting, hoeing, and watering vegetables and fruit in our parent's many gardens. We three younger brothers not yet in the mines had to help Mother prepare more than 500 jars of preserves, blueberries, pick-

les, sauerkraut, rabbit meat, beets, carrots, peas, beans, and tomatoes yearly. To clean all those jars, we partially filled them with
lead shot from 12- or 16-gauge shells and shook each jar; this
cleaned out all the muck before we washed them in hot, sudsy
water and a cold rinse. We also helped Dad make beer, wine, and
moonshine for family consumption and for sale.

I owe my dad and mother a lot. They never, ever gave me
a penny, but every day they counted the kids to be sure we were
there. At age five, I was out on the streets selling newspapers for
pennies a day. You can't buy much comfort on that salary. But
bless them, they saw that I was fed, warm, and clothed (most of the
time with hand-me-downs from four older brothers), and that I
behaved and followed them to church.

The Inheritance

I had a beautiful pocket knife with one large blade and one
small blade. I heated up a piece of wire and burned my initials into
the imitation pearl handle: "J.D." I really treasured it. One Fathers'
Day, I had no money to purchase a gift for Dad, which I always did.
So I gave him the knife as a gift. He was obviously thrilled, and
treasured it all his life.

Dad whittled. Every spring and summer my mother would
put in her usual order to him for sharpened tall and short bean and
tomato poles, stakes of all kinds, sausage sticks, wooden stirrers,
row markers, and picket fences. He whittled all his life. In his last
year he whittled summer and winter in the warm, comfortable
basement of their tiny home where a wood-burning, 50-year-old
kitchen stove kept him comfortable. He whittled over a large nail
barrel. After he filled the barrel, Mother would use the shavings to
start the stove.

Sometime after his funeral, Mother started to use the shavings for the stove, taking out handfuls as necessary. When she came to the bottom, there it was — my "J.D." knife that he had used for forty-six years. Some months later I returned for a visit and Mother handed the knife to me and said, "This is what your dad left you." It was all the inheritance I got. No money, no stocks, no bonds, no property, no homes, no businesses, just a knife that I had given him. It was enough.

Tony

I was six years old when Anthony Gregor DeBevec, my eldest brother, came into my vision. He was an indefatigably kind iron ore miner with a flair for gentle persuasion, and a great teacher, not only of the piano and accordion, but in providing everyday solutions to his five brothers' problems. I never remember him swearing, cheating, fighting, arguing, or being unkind to anyone. In the Eastern European tradition, the father in the family relies on his firstborn son to mold obedience and respect in any following progeny. Tony assumed this mantle of responsibilities superbly.

He was only sixteen years old, probably a sophomore in high school, when my parents "commissioned" him to enter the mines. With five brothers under fourteen years of age, someone had to help feed and clothe them. So down the "Hole" he went at the Adams Mine on December 24, 1922, one day before his sixteenth birthday.

He worked in various levels from 100 to 1,400 feet underground from 1922 to 1929. He never cashed one paycheck during those years. He signed every check over to our mother to help support all of us for those seven years. If Mother gave him a small stipend for personal expenses that was fine; if not, that was fine too. Working in the dark, seeping underground was exhausting but he never complained. I remember so well when he came home from a backbreaking shift and I was "hired" to unlace his high-top leather boots for five cents a week. He could have done it himself, but he knew he was teaching me to earn my keep. If he worked a normal day, he made $4.44, a price that today's teens pay for a lunch at McDonald's — at their parents' expense!

In 1930 he married his beloved lovely wife, Frances. Ironically, the mines then closed down, leaving the newly married couple without any income. He supported himself in poorly paid odd jobs until the mines reopened offering a meager $3.15 a day. He eventually went to open-pit mining operations where he became an explosives expert and eventually a supervisor of the whole pit.

Aggie

Most people cannot claim saints for brothers or sisters. A few may lay claim to one, perhaps, but I was lucky — I had two: my eldest brother Tony and my saintly sister, Aggie, the eldest child in the family. I have always felt I had a special place in Aggie's heart and that we had a loving rapport that didn't exist between her and our other brothers, though she was kind, considerate, and benevolent to them, too. She was my second mother and that was no easy task, for I was a rambunctious, ambitious, hell-bent kid from the time I was born. But, through all my shenanigans, Aggie remained kind, understanding, and loving.

My parents were loving and supportive, too, and I worshiped them, but my mother and dad were extremely busy trying to put food on the table and clothes on the backs of seven children on a poor miner's salary. If Dad wasn't slaving in the mine and Mother in the house, they were forced to be absent from home clearing, digging, grubbing, hoeing, and watering patches of land they borrowed or rented to raise food for our ever-hungry stomachs: lettuce, cabbage, beets, potatoes, tomatoes, peas, spinach, endive, cucumbers, carrots, pumpkins, squash, radishes, kohlrabi, turnips, rutabagas, corn, beans, spinach; and wild blueberries and our own strawberries and dandelions for wine by the gallon.

Meanwhile, someone had to keep the kids in line, and that someone was Aggie. At the age of eighteen, she married John Klemencic, another miner and an absolute prince of a man. My folks "restructured" our Summit Street home and rented the second floor to Aggie and her new husband. That kept her close at hand. (It also meant that we six brothers had to relinquish our bedrooms. So three boys slept in one of Aggie's rooms upstairs, two slept on our sleeper sofa downstairs, and I slept on the floor in the corner behind the upright Isinglass wood-burning parlor stove. And so it remained for years.)

Through the early years of her marriage, Aggie comforted and healed my physical, moral, and religious wounds. She provided a medical, physical, and spiritual oasis.

After marrying John, she bore her only child, her son Bob. It was a difficult birth that nearly took her from us. I remember how Mother gathered Dad and all of us boys and led us for half an hour praying on our knees outside Aggie's bedroom.

Aggie bore with migraine headaches that were a painful part of every day of her life until she died at age eighty-three. The pain was so intense that sometimes she would retire to her bedroom, close the door, and wait without rest until it passed. There were no drugs in 1925 to combat this malady except aspirin and cold towel packs. Yet I never heard her complain or bemoan the fact that this was her lot in life.

Aggie served as our doctor. Her treatments were generally old-fashioned European folk remedies, cures that would amuse parents today — but they worked! I remember a few of her mirac-

ulous potions. For a sore throat, she would have us swallow men-
tholatum, or rub it on our throat and into our nostrils, and then
wrap our necks in a washed woolen sock. In emergencies, the sock
might be unwashed!

She treated cuts, bruises, and abrasions with a dabble of
Dad's homemade moonshine. For chest colds, she applied layers of
cloth soaked in mustard to the chest. For an infected toe nail, she
dug a certain weed from our garden, which she pounded into a
pulp and inserted into a pouch-like cloth that she tied around the
toe; or, she would cover the toe with unrisen bread dough to draw
out the pus. Aggie had a cure for every ailment.

Later in life, I would return to visit her with my family.
Cheerful Aggie would always have spent hours cooking and baking in anticipation of our arrival, an unbelievable spread of my
favorite Slovenian food: blood sausage from Primozich's store,
smoked pork and beef sausages (klobase) from Postudensek's in
Leonadis, Kislo Zelje (homemade warm sauerkraut), and a superb
dish we all called "minestra" of sauerkraut, beans, and potatoes all
mashed hot in a pot. And I will never forget the Slovenian nut roll
and apple potica (strudel) and krofe, which were delightful fried
strips of sweet dough.

Rex

Ruler! Master! Leader! King!

King he was. A huge, overpowering master of his domain,
706 Summit Street, Rex was a gigantic brown and white St.
Bernard. He weighed more than I did at the age of ten. How could
a poor iron ore miner and his family afford that venerable, most-
respected dog? My dad got him for nothing from someone who
couldn't afford to feed him any longer. I asked my dad, if the generous donor could not afford the food necessary to sustain a 110-

pound miniature horse, how could he? I have cherished his answer for almost seventy years: "Never refuse a gift from anyone. You must not offend the giver by intimating that the gift is not good enough for you. Never worry, the Lord will provide."

I thought that was one helluva big working project for the Lord. But Rex never went hungry. There weren't many scraps from our table, but we managed to collect enough scraps from other tables in the neighborhood to feed him. We conducted a daily, door-to-door collection ritual. Rex served as a guardian for the whole block, so all of the families in our area accepted him as a feeding responsibility.

Baby buggies were a rarity in those days, so mothers would assemble their young ones on the "boulevard" — a four-foot stretch of tree-lined grass between the sidewalk and the street. If there were four babies from four families, Rex showed no partiality. If anyone attempted to touch a baby, he growled, not an earthshaking roar, but a slow "Grring" warning. He was also a sentinel for neighboring homes. He could hear someone entering a gate or yard from as far away as six homes on either side of ours. Then he'd sound out his alarm.

He was never allowed in the house. His station was outside the back door, where he slept. The nearest thing to comfort he had in severe winter weather, when it would get down to 60 degrees below, was to sleep on the back porch.

Dad was very inventive. He had only a second-grade education, but he could build anything. He built a huge wooden sled for Rex to pull. It was four feet wide and six feet long with large, stationary rear runners and swivel front runners. He fashioned a leather harness and Rex became a wood hauler. He was as strong as an ox and could pull a very heavy load.

Most families could not afford to buy coal for heating so we used wood almost exclusively for heat in the winter months.

Our family, like most, spent many summer hours cutting, hauling, splitting, and stacking huge piles of wood in our yards — like squirrels storing nuts for the winter. We would go up the street to Pugel's Hill, past the cow pasture and the ravine, where we would chop out and unearth tree stumps, cut windfalls, and place them in a pile, intending to come back in the winter to haul them home. The piles stayed there all summer, untouched. Other families built piles too. No one touched them. Everyone knew that some family would need their precious pile of wood to heat a hungry stove and a cold bedroom of kids — and honored that need.

Then, in the winter, we kids would hitch up Rex and take off for the wilderness four blocks away, near Fabiola Bluff and the pond. We always mixed work with pleasure, taking our clamp-on skates, building a roaring fire where we baked potatoes black in the coals, slapping each other around, and showing off our skating prowess. Come dusk we would load Rex's sled with wood and head for home. Often we'd load up several neighborhood kids and Rex would take them on an unforgettable ride through the streets.

One day he was not at his usual guardian position near our back door. This was a grave concern for all the families. He was missing for two days before he showed up with a heavy broken wire about eight feet long tied to his collar. He was very sick. He had been led away and poisoned. Dad and my brothers worked feverishly to hurry his convalescence by concocting their own remedy to force him to throw up the poison. One of the ingredients was gun powder. Through the grace of God, Rex recovered.

We didn't do any undercover work to find out who the culprits were, but it had to have been someone living near us who knew Rex well enough to command him to follow. The detectives in our family deduced that Rex's barking was hurting the moonshine operations in the neighborhood.

A few weeks later he was gone again, this time forever. He

never returned. The King was dead. God save the King.

Cracker Jack

Christmas to most adults and children means a towering Christmas tree with a plethora of ornaments and a myriad of shimmering lights, the bottom overflowing with ribbon-wrapped gifts and money. And children wide-eyed in anticipation of an avalanche of toys from Santa.

But during the 1920s, this was not so for most mining families in northern Minnesota. I was too young to understand why we all had so little, even food. There may have been a strike, or the coal bills were extremely high, or wages were lower than a snake's belly, or miners constructing their first homes were inundated with bills for construction, or food costs that had spiraled.

In any event, frugality became an obsession for many poor families, including our family of nine. For some years, miners' families could afford few gifts and toys during Christmas — and sometimes none. I remember very well when our family had none.

But we always had a beautiful tree. We could walk into the woods six blocks from our home and cut "the perfect tree" and haul it home on a sled and be back in an hour. The tree was set up bare and remained bare, except for a few wax candles attached to the branches with clips. However, lighting them was prohibited unless someone in the family was there to ensure the tree would not catch fire, so we used them sparingly.

The year I was seven, five-year-old Louis and I still believed in Santa Claus. The whole family went to midnight mass on Christmas Eve. Then we got up together on Christmas morning and went to see if Santa had left anything under our tree. However, the nine of us stared at the barren base of the tree. Santa had evidently missed our house completely. No presents. None! This was not a shock to the older siblings who had ceased to believe in Santa long before. But Louie and I stood transfixed, although without tears, complaints, or tantrums.

After all, we had been good kids! How could we be bad? We had nothing to be bad with.

But my mom and dad and the five older children had decided that Louie and I should not be deprived of a belief in Santa. With a sudden babble of voices, they all began telling us not to be disappointed, because Santa may have missed the tree — but not the house. They said, "Let's all go together to search the house."

So, imitating Christ's parents looking for a place of rest 1,922 years earlier, we all systematically searched through every room in the house, not for a "room in an inn" but for "some present within." We started upstairs and took a long inspection of each of the five rooms and closets, even the bathroom. And after each room, sighs were heard from all: "No, not here. No, not here. Maybe the next room." I don't know about Louie, but I thought, "Sweet Jesus, this is going to take all day." Then, downstairs — and after a thorough search of every room, there was only one place left: our back porch.

There we stood in our night clothes, on a porch that was surely 20 degrees below zero. I had a gut feeling that a miracle like Christ's birth was about to happen because, like Mary and Joseph, "there was no other place for us to go." After inspecting every nook and cranny, we came to an overturned galvanized wash tub in a corner and I was offered the privilege of lifting it. And there we found Santa's Christmas gifts to Louie and me: two five-cent boxes of Cracker Jack!

However, the story doesn't end there. And it probably never will, as long as there are children of children of children of friends of ours. Some years later I told the story to the children of some of our friends. The story spread among other friends, so they called on me to repeat it to their children many times.

One night we were invited to the home of Mr. and Mrs. Ivan Sand for a Christmas party and I told the Cracker Jack story to their three children. The tale of poverty impressed and moved many children, but none like Jennifer, their five-year-old daughter, who listened with tears rolling down her cheeks.

I thought nothing more of it. But the Cracker Jack story never left Jennie Sand. I retired in 1975 and left to live in Phoenix, Arizona where we spent all of our Christmases from then on. And the first Christmas I was there in 1975, I received a small package in the mail from Jennie — two boxes of Cracker Jack!

Jennie and I kept up a steady correspondence during her progression through high school, college, and a teaching position in Albertsville, Minnesota, and her marriage to a great guy, Mark Haller. And gentle readers, Jennie sent two or three packages of Cracker Jack to me in Phoenix every Christmas for twenty years! All those years, the postage alone was many times the total price of the two boxes of Cracker Jack in 1922.

For twenty years, we spent six months of summer in Little Falls, Minnesota and Toronto, and all our Christmases in Phoenix. However, in 1995, we spent our first Christmas away from Phoenix at our condo in Toronto. On December 19, 1995, a package for Christmas arrived there: three boxes of Cracker Jack from Benjamin Haller, age one-and-a-half — Jennie's son!

The Autographed Baseball

I once won a super-duper prize — a genuine, big-league baseball autographed by the immortal Babe Ruth. Wow! That was the ultimate!

I was extremely fortunate to have held onto it in a home

with six sons and only two small bedrooms. With so little privacy, how do you hold on to a precious baseball? About five years later, when we built a nice two-story home at St. Mary's Lake nearby, my mother insisted on a simple red brick fireplace. I don't remember it ever being lighted and the only thing on the shallow mantle was my Babe Ruth ball. It nested in a wooden cup with a stem. It looked great and everyone respected it and what it stood for. How many kids win a ball like that?

Then one day it was gone!

Eventually it came out. My brother two years my junior and some of his pals were playing baseball in an adjoining lot and lost their only ball. Who could possibly afford a new one? So my brother took my revered Babe Ruth ball.

If no one owned a bat, they'd use a two-by-four or a steel pipe or a heavy tree branch. The ball took a beating. So it never made it back. Too bad. I wonder how much it would be worth today.

Well, how many poor kids get to hit a $5,000 baseball?

Pugel's Hill

Eveleth's population was about 5,000 in 1920. We lived on the upper block of Summit Street, near the summit for which the street was named. At the end of the block the town ended at a rumpled hill one block wide and two blocks long — Pugel's Hill, after a family who lived adjacent to it. Their dad, father of twelve, was killed in the womb of the iron ore mine when he was around forty years old.

The hill was our Mecca. We kids came here almost daily for our summer and winter sports activities. We took days to form a ski track down the hill, and hours of fruitful labor to pack snow to form a ski jump. We made our own skis of used barrel staves to which we nailed leather straps to hold our feet. We would climb that enormous hill to the top, get our contraptions set down on the trail, crouch, take a deep breath and shove off, the wind biting our scarf-hidden faces as we hurled downward.

At the bottom of Pugel's Hill lay a small, weed-infested pond. In the summer, it made a place to swim fully clothed, since we only wore a pair of J.C. Penney bib overalls and were always barefoot. Or we built and floated a simple raft. In the winter, we skated there, building a fire, and baking potatoes jet black in the hot coals. We were poor, but we all had a huge bin of potatoes in our cellars. We didn't have anything resembling modern skates. Ours were simple blades that clamped on and screwed to leather-top rubber-bottom boots with a key.

At Pugel's Hill, we learned how to break a leg without really trying. Beyond the hill, a huge pit had been carved out to furnish sand for street and highway construction and repair. In the winter, when it was not being used, tons of soft, glistening snow fell or drifted in, covering the bottom and rising many feet. We would walk back twenty feet from the edge, run toward the pit and leap into the deep blanket of snow. We usually hit bottom. And since we were only four to five feet tall, we had to dig our way out. Unfortunately we had a few broken arms or legs, and the wrath of parents made it off limits — but just for a week or so, and then we were back at it again. You can't keep a good thing away from kids.

Castles

Parallel to the cow pasture, the land dipped for a long way, thick with birch, tamarack, spruce, pine, and poplar trees. In this secret valley, we dug square pits in the ground six feet by six feet square and six feet deep — our secret underground castles. We furnished these with all the refined ambiance and amenities necessary to sustain and please young explorers of the wilderness — three blocks from home. We scavenged boards, nails, stoves, stove pipes, two-by-fours, shingles, firewood, fourth-hand furniture, rugs, and of course, potatoes.

When we left after a day of fun, we would remove the chimneys and cover the roofs and trap doors with green sod, so no one would discover our castles. But sometimes when we returned after a day or two, we'd find that some culprits had desecrated our "homes," ripped our concealed roofs, smashed our stove and furniture. We forgot that we operated our community of underground town houses within a social stratum and a pecking order. Those who had poor camps or none at all envied ours, and so they destroyed them.

As I look back over the last sixty-five years, we as a people have learned very little about tolerance and envy and less about our tendency toward destructiveness. But being poor (only in material things) in the 1920s created a great advantage. In our early years, we learned not to be too dependent on our parents or our siblings or on anyone else. We had to learn to work hard, be creative, and imaginative, and to have faith enough to follow His rules.

Our whole neighborhood, including Pugel's Hill, was not more than one mile square at most. However, out of this precious piece of land we children of poor Slovenian, Croatian, Serbian, Italian, Finnish, Norwegian, and Swedish immigrants grew older, wiser, and kinder as we amused and amazed ourselves. We loved and laughed and played and built, creating a happy life from nothing.

Halloween

In 1929, all the iron ore mining towns on the Iron Range in northern Minnesota clustered together within a few miles. In our area, a railroad that had only one electrically operated car connected towns like Virginia, Eveleth, Genoa, and Gilbert for a fare of five cents. We would go down to the small, outdoor-stop station about a hundred yards from Pugel's Hill to watch the trains stop, pick up passengers, and amble onward. While waiting for the next train, we would dream up ideas for our annual Halloween misadventures. We never went trick-or-treating. We felt our lot in life was to create a Halloween experience that would shock but never hurt anybody.

Early one Halloween night, we spread hundreds of dead frogs, grasshoppers, and earthworms on the track, exactly where we knew the train would stop. When it did, the passengers got on, the train started — and then stopped. It started again, inching forward. Then it slipped, the wheels spinning.

After a few minutes, the driver got out and said, "What the hell is happening?" Then the conductor got out and said, "What the hell is happening?" All the passengers got out and said, "What the hell is happening?" But we, in the darkness of Halloween night, hunched behind clumps of bushes fifty feet away, grinned and chuckled with glee because we knew "what the hell was happening." It was quite a sight — and quite a night.

Competing With Cows

Parallel to Pugel's Hill ran a strip of land with long wire fences that guarded the cow pasture provided free by the city. A steady parade of cows was driven back and forth daily to roam and nibble. I remember being paid five cents a day to drive some neighbors' cows up and back. This bovine Valhalla contained huge holes that looked like bomb craters, about twelve feet in diameter. They were "test holes" created by mining engineers searching for possible deposits of ore. Found worthless, they were left unfilled, except by rains and underground currents that filled them with water that did not recede. Here the cows drank and bathed.

But we kids considered these our private swimming holes. So, often we competed to see who could get in first, the cows or us. We always made a celebration by building a fire and roasting potatoes with their skins on, or corn with husks on in the hot coals. Both came out jet black but what a feast — what a life!

Hockey

As kids, hockey was the stuff of life. It was full of heroes and stories. It taught us excellence, teamwork, and competition. I have always thought back about how hockey was more than a game for us, more than getting a puck into the net. It was getting something from life into the net. A great game to learn from.

The game of hockey was born in Canada and introduced to the U.S. in Eveleth, my childhood home in northern Minnesota. Eveleth nurtured and grew the "fastest game in the world" and created hockey players who achieved fame all over the country.

Eveleth is now home to the U.S. Hockey Hall of Fame. Our high school coach, Cliff Thompson, is enshrined there. Disabled in World War I, Cliff never played a single game of hockey. Yet, as high school coach from 1920 to 1958, his teams won 534 games, lost twenty-six games, and tied nine. Between 1948 and 1951, Coach Thompson's teams won seventy-eight straight victories. They were state champions five years in a row. He sent eleven players to the NHL. Four of them, all born and trained in Eveleth, are enshrined with him in the Hall of Fame: Frank Brimsek, goalie for the Boston Bruins; Mike Karakas, goalie for the Chicago Black Hawks; Sam Lopresti, goalie for the Chicago Black Hawks; and John Mariucci, defense man for the Chicago Black Hawks.

The Eveleth hockey Hippodrome was really something!

An open-air stadium, it was not. It had a roof to prevent the sub-zero temperatures making "stiffs" out of us while we watched and to keep falling snow out of our eyes so we could see the game.

The Hippodrome was gigantic, especially to preteen youngsters. It looked like a colossal Quonset hut with its semicircular roof curving down to form the sides. In retrospect, I think it was a block long and a half block wide and 50 feet high. It was built of wood with a series of windows and an entrance on the east side, and one door on both the north and south sides with one large window near the top on those sides. It was one helluva pile of wood.

There the Eveleth Rangers, a National Hockey League team, clashed with the likes of the Chicago Black Hawks, Boston Bruins, Toronto Maple Leafs, Montreal Canadians, and others. Most of the hockey players on all the teams were Canadians. All the players on the Eveleth team originally came from Canada. Some hockey stars I remember were Moose Goheen, Eddie Rodden, Vic des Jardines, Charles Connacher, Ching Johnson, and Eddie Johnson. All the NHL teams came to Minnesota by bus or train. Because our rail lines were insufficient, they had to take a bus to Eveleth. They always stayed at the Park Hotel on Adams Avenue — our only hotel — which had small rooms and large communal bathrooms.

Hockey was an expensive sport for a youngster to watch. A child's ticket cost five cents, a sum we could not afford. We found a few ways to get in free, but it was tough.

Way #1 We would go to the Park Hotel and wait outside in sub-zero cold for the visiting players to come out after their dinner. With luck, we could get in free by carrying a visiting player's bag and his hockey stick to the game. They allowed every player "one kid," but that meant only twelve kids got to accompany the players on their ceremonial walk the four blocks to the rink at the

Eveleth Hippodrome.

Way #2 We would go to the entrance of the Hippodrome and stand in the bitterly cold weather hoping some rich banker, lawyer, businessman, doctor, or mining owner or executive would feel sorry for us poor miners' sons and spend five cents to let one of us in. With some exceptions, this was not successful.

Way #3 We would sneak in through a small window near the roof, kept open to allow air to flow out. Getting to this window presented a real challenge, but if you made it, eager people inside would gladly drag you in. We used ladders from sympathetic miners whose homes were adjacent to the Hippodrome.

Way #4 We would go down to the Hippodrome late in the afternoon, hours before the game, with a small shovel. We would then dig a hole through the frozen ground somewhere along the foundation of the long west wall, an arduous task. We would dig it only deep enough to squeeze our small bodies under the wooden base. It took a long time, but we didn't have to worry about anyone seeing us because the west wall faced a mining pit. Then we covered the hole very gingerly with snow to wait for the game. But police officers patrolled the outside constantly, so we'd have to wait for them to turn the corner before we began uncovering our holes and squeezing ourselves in. Then we could scurry to a seat somewhere inside to witness the fastest game on earth. Generally, we had no problems.

But once, as I started to crawl through my private hole, my pants and jacket got caught on the jagged wood. I couldn't move forward or backward without tearing my clothes. I was very concerned because I had only seconds in which to elude the law. Suddenly I felt a terrific blow on my backside and then a growl: "Utsah you name?" I recognized the voice of Mr. Angerelli, the Italian police officer — a kind but a judicious gentleman. I yelled, "Joey." He yelled, "Eh, Jovie a whoo." I yelled, "Joey DeBevec."

He yelled, "Eh, mama mia, datsa poor Anton's bambino" And then he yelled these immortal words "Jovie, go heen or go hout or go home!" He rapped me again hard on my keister and as I jerked loose, he grabbed me by the seat of my pants and shoved me in!

Water Tower

Our home on Summit Street was near the highest point in the city, which was built on a large, mesa-like hill. The next street to ours was Harrison, and the top of Harrison was the highest point in the city. Of course, that was where the city built a solid steel water tank, ten to fourteen stories high on four huge supporting legs. Steel bars crisscrossed the legs all the way up to the bottom of the tank.

Climbing the water tower took a lot of guts. One false step and you would meet your maker in seconds. If you could climb all the way up, you would arrive at a trap door. This gave access to a circular walk with a four-foot high fence circling the bottom of the tank. Then came the "brave clincher" — an unprotected steel ladder that jutted out at a dangerous angle to the rim of the roof. Another trap door led to the rim. Then a steel ladder bolted into the pointed roof climbed to the top where a huge steel ball capped the tower. If you touched that ball, you had conquered the world. I did, at age ten.

Schnoppa

My closest friend in the neighborhood was Wilho Walkama, a Finn. Everyone called him "Schnoppa." His family had lost his father, a miner, at an early age. The family had a difficult time. We all did, but their case was worse. His family could give him little support, so the poor kid, sixth of seven children, had to fend for himself. They had some family devotion, but little discipline and, unfortunately, no religious activity. Schnoppa was really a wild one, but not mean or destructive. He was a loyal and honest friend who would do anything for me, and I felt just as strongly about him.

I was attracted to him because of his desire to earn money without violating any laws. I felt an equal desire not to burden the rest of my family. We were always successful. We were constant companions.

One day in June 1930, I got the idea that the two of us should go to Chicago, a thousand miles away. We had no money. We'd have to leave with no luggage, just the clothes on our backs — jeans, shoes, a shirt, and a light jacket. We had to keep our plan in utmost secrecy, since our parents would never approve. Somehow we would have to work for food. We had no travel plans and only a vague idea where Chicago was. We had no train or bus tickets. At fifteen, we were too young to hitchhike. We'd have to "flip" freight cars on the railroads, like hobos.

But the Chicago World's Fair was on — a gigantic, once-in-a-lifetime opportunity. I knew little about it, except that people from all over the world would be there. If we got there, we could always stay at the home of my Aunt Teta and Uncle Gregor Gregorich. Of course, I didn't have their permission and they had no idea that we were about to visit them. I did know approximately where they lived, but I didn't know if they had a telephone.

Two days after I got the idea, we two skinny kids who had never been more than four miles from home took off for the end of the world — Chicago — with a total of $2.30 between us and without telling anyone in our families. We walked first to Fayal Road, which led out of town, then hitched a ride to Superior, Wisconsin, about 60 miles away.

We had seen many five-cent cowboy movies so we thought

we knew how to get on and off a moving freight train. We walked to the railroad yards, which we had never been in before. There we met a lot of railroad bums who were going anywhere, everywhere, and nowhere. They were good teachers who warned us about the perils of jumping on and off moving cars. They also warned us to watch out for the "bulls" — railroad police in every yard in America who would arrest anyone trying to get a free train ride. 1930 was the year after the stock market crash, and railroad yards everywhere were inundated with bums trying to get free lifts.

Only six hours from home, we were already learning the intricacies of getting from point A to point B at no cost. The bum veterans also coached us to look for trains that sported two white flags on the front of the engine. These "fast freights" ran twice as fast as the usual freights.

The constant vigilance of railroad bulls made it very difficult to board the trains while they were stopped in the yards. To flip a freight, you had to get out of the yards and hop onto the train while it slowly picked up speed as it left the yard. Soon we were veterans of hitting the rungs, climbing to the top of the car, and crossing the cat walks. When we came to a flatbed filled with machinery, steel parts and lumber, we settled down for our free ride.

We made our first stop in Yville, Wisconsin, a huge switching yard where trains came for water, coal, and supplies at all hours. We were hungry, so we went to small homes near the tracks, asking to do odd jobs for food. Luckily, at our second stop a kindly woman needed some wood chopped. We did it for an hour or so. She gave us bags of food and twenty-five cents each. We now had $2.80 in our common fund. Then we veteran railroad bums returned to the Yville yards and easily flipped a train with a double white flag to Chicago. The cars were filled with bums on top, underneath, on oil tankers, in empty box cars, on flatbeds —

one big traveling family. Schnoppa and I felt genuinely initiated into the society of the railroad bums. We were very proud.

As we approached Chicago, the freeloaders sternly warned us: "Don't get in the yards. The Chicago bulls are the worst in the nation. There's no simple slap on the wrist. They'll send you right to jail." So, with hand-signs, we learned how to jump off as the train neared the Chicago yards. Dusting ourselves off, we found ourselves in a suburb called Cicero. We all congregated in a "jungle." (These were dry streambeds under a bridge or secluded dense woods or bushes.) Here, in complete privacy, the true railroad bum community started to hum, everyone sharing news, taking notes, exchanging jokes, and sharing food. Fires were lit to heat food in cans suspended with clumsy contraptions. We were glad to learn all we could from these "professors." They told us to tell people that we were lost hicks from Minnesota, and since we looked hungry and skinny, they would immediately deluge us with assistance in transportation and food.

Once we got into the city, we learned to wait for a street car loaded with people all the way to the rear door, on the steps on the outside, and hanging on the hand rails. Then the poor ticket collector, pinned against the windows inside, would never get to us. When the streetcar emptied, if we needed a transfer, we would say "You forgot to give me one" or "I lost mine" or "I'm from Minnesota and I didn't think I needed one." (Saying you were from Minnesota always evoked immediate sympathy because Chicagoans thought that all Minnesotans were mistreated Indians who needed compassion.)

So we hustled our way through the big city. I knew only that my uncle and aunt lived on West 22nd Place near Cermak Road. We finally got there after many free transfers. My aunt and uncle were in the same condition as my parents in Minnesota must have been then: shocked, furious, frightened — but deliriously happy. Aunt Teta called my family to assure them that we were O.K.

My aunt and uncle had no spare rooms so we slept on the floor in our traveling clothes. We ate like lions and slept like bears, exhausted from the trip. Recovered, we lost little time being assimilated in the neighborhood, and were soon enjoying life with other teens in that ethnic section of the city.

After a few days of that paradise, we decided to seek out the World's Fair on the shore of Lake Michigan. A five-cent street car fare took us to the entrance. We checked the admission prices — too high for us. But Schnoppa had a nose for uncovering entrances to protected places. Some blocks from the main entrance, near the shoreline, he discovered a slight dip in the ground under the fence. We crawled through, dusted ourselves off, and walked to the midway.

What a monumental display! The pride and progress of dozens of foreign countries! After a quick tour, we decided that somewhere in this conglomeration of exhibits, we could find someone who needed our special talents — and would pay us for them.

General Motors had a demonstration of the new shatterproof windshield. A man showed slides and gave an interesting five-minute talk before a crowd on the effectiveness of the new windshield. At the end, he would ask someone in the audience to come to the podium and throw a regular baseball at a new windshield from about 40 feet away. If the thrower was accurate, the impact would cause fissures all over but the glass would not shatter. The chosen throwers often missed the windshield, which ruined the GM man's presentation. I waited for my chance, and after a steady parade of misses, I walked up to him and said, "Fella, you're hurting your act. I can hit that windshield ten times out of ten." (I played American Legion baseball and had a good throwing arm.)

He said, "You're cocksure, so I'll give you a try." After his next presentation, he handed me the ball and said, "Here, skinny, and I hope you're good enough."

I said, "Watch this!"

Splat! Bull's eye. He really looked surprised and said, "Hang around for the next go-around and I'll give you a buck."

I was suddenly wealthy. I worked for him until his shift was over and he left, giving me a few bucks.

Schnoppa had left after I was hired and returned to tell me he had found a job setting white wooden milk bottles in a pyramid at a gallery that sold three baseball throws for 25 cents — "Knock 'em down with three balls and you get a Kewpie doll." He told me where it was and to join him later.

We had planned to stay only one day, but now that we were successful entrepreneurs, we decided to stay two days. We didn't want the hassle and expense of returning to my aunt's or the risk of having to pay admission if the crack in the fence became plugged when the police checked the fence. So we decided to stay inside the fair overnight. We found a safe spot near the shoreline with bushes and boulders to hide us, curled up in our clothes, and went to sleep. We forgot to tell my aunt and uncle that we were staying over for another day, and wouldn't be home for supper that night.

We spent our second day at the World's Fair unemployed and visiting the wonders of the exhibits. High school textbooks were never as educational as that. There were dozens of entertainment centers and a constant carnival atmosphere, with stage shows everywhere. Sally Rand made her debut dancing in the nude with nothing but ostrich fans, but we couldn't afford to see her. Too bad.

We finally had our fill and it was time to go home. We had fulfilled our destiny. We returned to my uncle and aunt's, made a hasty goodbye, and began our trip back home to Minnesota. We returned the same way we came, making the same stops, with the same railroad paying our fare, and facing the same dangers. But this time we returned to Minnesota as worldly-wise travelers. Eveleth, Minnesota would never again be the same for Schnoppa and me. We returned to the wild enthusiasm of our families, as if we had risen from the dead. I brought gifts: two brown and white sea shells that cost a quarter apiece. Carved in the tops were "Aggie" and "Mother."

Poverty . . . Then and Now

To me, one of the most exciting things in the world was being poor.

According to the Toronto Star, poverty is the most important cause of youthful bad behavior. Children from low-income families have less esteem and more behavioral problems than children from wealthier families.

Horse manure! No one was poorer than my friends and I were. But we were only poor in material things. In our town, everyone who wasn't a miner was rich. We had people who acted like the Kennedys, Roosevelts, and Rockefellers in Eveleth. But their kids were the ones with problems and their families were just as disgraceful with their wealth. They sent their children to the best schools, but we were street-smart. We handled our problems better than they did because we had to solve them ourselves. The rich kids had their problems solved for them.

Growing up in an iron ore miner's family was a unique experience, especially in an eastern European immigrant's household. We had solid, traditional family rules handed down from generation to generation. Now, seventy years later, many families have become disintegrated and dysfunctional because they dropped those family values, rules, and ethics as no longer necessary. I still hold on to mine and still use them to influence my Canadian and American children who are in their forties and fifties. Why discard a good set of behavioral ethics?

In my time the father was king of the family and he ruled with a gentle but firm hand, the same hand that crossed the seat of many pants when it was necessary. His word was law. The eldest son assumed command in case of his death, or if he became ill, or pressures became too great for him.

Everyone in the family had to get a job. I don't remember anyone in our family ever being unemployed — even in the worst of the Depression years. And everyone, on their hours away from employment, worked on some family endeavor to help sustain us. Each had to share his or her talents — cultivate vegetable and fruit gardens on rented lots, cut and store wood, repair everything that needed fixing, hunt for game to feed the nine hungry children, slop the hogs, feed the cow.

I can just hear the objections already: "Well, we can't do those things today!"

No, I agree, but I can immediately think of as many activities as above to replace them in the 1990's. And if you can't, my sympathy goes out to you.

Everyone in a family should share his earnings. That is the way immigrant families still operate today. I remember with complete clarity that every Saturday night after pay day my mother would sit on a kitchen chair, and spread wide her apron. All six sons, before leaving the house to pursue their own social activities, would drop their contributions to the family in her lap. Even I, at age six, earning little more than ten cents a day, threw in at least a nickel. We all settled individually with her what would be a fair offering according to what we earned. And we wouldn't cheat our own mother. She always had God looking over her shoulder — and ours!

There must be a better way!

"It's no shame to be poor or ignorant, but it's a
damn shame to stay that way."

Joey

IN MY YOUTH, I RAN AND JUMPED AROUND and worked like
a stud cricket on a hot stove lid. From ages five to eighteen, I was
into anything and everything to make a buck — or a quarter — or
a nickel — or a penny. I peddled papers, sold Christmas cards,
picked ground pine boughs and made them into Christmas wreaths
that I sold, sold minnows and grasshoppers, cut Christmas trees
and sold them, made floats for parades, picked up used copper and
aluminum and rags to sell to the Jewish rag merchant who came
every Tuesday, printed signs on white cardboard like "Men's
Toilet," "Ladies Toilet," "For Sale," "Closed," "Open," etc. for
business and professional men, worked as a field hand on neighboring farms, washed cars, searched garbage cans for canceled
postage stamps, rope, copper, aluminum and other materials and
sold them, played the violin and string bass in our family orchestra, sawed logs and used telephone poles for customers, helped
deliver tons of California grapes to homes for winemaking, picked
dandelions in the fields for neighbors to make wine and salads,
delivered homemade wine and whiskey for neighbors, delivered
groceries in a horse-drawn sleigh, baby-sat for neighbor children,

house-sat for neighbors' homes, painted, worked in thistle gangs with hoes to eradicate obnoxious Canadian thistles, fought forest fires, killed rats for a bounty, trapped rabbits and sold them, drove the neighbors' cows to the pasture, entered sports contests for prizes, won yo-yo contests, sold magazine and newspaper subscriptions, sold wooden blocks from disbanded street car tracks, helped our parish priest, Father Leskovic, teach Catechism, hired out as an escort for proms, repaired hockey sticks, made and sold barrel-stave skis, cleaned cattle and pig barns, sold "Rose Bud" Vaseline door-to-door, built confectionery stands and sold Eskimo Pies, candy, pop, and gum at sports events, circuses, and special community events, cleaned pots and pans for the Kneebone family every Saturday, planted trees, sang in the Presbyterian choir on McKinley Avenue, worked in a pop factory on Jackson Street, served as a "gofer" for NHL Hockey players in Eveleth for games, carried their sticks and bags into the Hippodrome, organized neighborhood "carnivals," helped milk the neighbors' cows, washed store windows, ran errands, shoveled snow, made and sold kites, ushered at the Regent Theater, hauled ashes from neighbors' kitchen stoves and furnaces to their gardens for fertilizer or to their garbage cans, lighted fires for Jewish people on their Sabbath, cleaned hockey and curling rinks, worked as a painter for schools during the summer. And I was always paid.

It Was So Cold That . . .

Northern Minnesota has "nine months of snow and sleet and three months of bad skiing." Many below-zero mornings, as I looked at the smoke from chimneys in warm homes, I would wonder what I was doing at that hour when other children my age were snuggled in bed under layers of quilts for another three or four hours. Were they right? Was I wrong? After all, there were only seven other preteen newspaper nuts like myself covering all the routes in town.

And before leaving home at 4:30 a.m. to pick up my papers a mile away, I had to prepare the kitchen stove for my mother. She had to get up minutes after I left to make breakfast and lunch buckets for my dad and brothers who had the early-morning shift at the mines. So every night before I crawled into bed, I would chop fine slivers of cedar for kindling and then split dry pieces of birch for the heavy fire. I'd stack them all in the wood box next to the wood-burning kitchen range, so Mother would have a goodly supply before I left for my newspaper duties. I'd fill the grates with birch bark, cedar kindling and birch logs, light them and leave so Mother had a warm kitchen to slave in.

November through April, I had to brace myself for the Arctic blast outside. Blizzards never bothered me; even if you can't see ten feet in it, a snow-driven blizzard is never cold. But, dear people, when you can hear the crunch of your boots in the hard-packed snow and you're wearing three layers of caps — beware! It's a killing 50 degrees below. In a blizzard with vision only good for three feet in front of you, you could get lost traveling a block. I remember farmers who were found dead trying to get to the barn from the house because they lost their direction.

I remember it being 62 degrees below (no wind chill factor, the paper said). Since all my clothes were "hand-me-downs" from four older brothers, I had to rely on castoffs to protect myself from freezing to death. In that weather, walking two blocks with an ear exposed would mean the end of the ear! I wore five or six hand-me-down-rags. I wrapped my feet in potato-sack strippings and wore leather-top bottom-rubber boots. I wore long underwear with a flap in the back and oversized sweaters. I wore two tassel caps covered with a leather sheep-lined Charles Lindbergh aviator cap, a gift from our family doctor and a prize for any kid who owned one. I wrapped my face with a scarf so just my eyes were exposed. Often I stopped to get my hands out of two woolen liners and leather buckskin mitts so I could melt the ice on my eyelids with my warm fingers. Then I had to be quick to get my fingers back unfrozen into the mitts. I must have been a sight. However, very few people were up at that hour to see.

Bratulich's Bakery

    I had to walk ten blocks to the George Pappas newsstand where I would pick up my papers to deliver to my 100 customers. The Greyhound bus that delivered the Tribune to all the iron range cities was often late, stalled, stuck, or snowbound, so I had to wait in the cold, dark morning. But I never worried about freezing to death because I had a warm harbor: August Bratulich's bakery. He often saw me outside in the frighteningly cold darkness and invited me into his bakery, which was open twenty-four hours a day, since they sold all day and baked all night. The warmth of the ovens iced the huge display windows, so the inside was invisible. But they never locked the door. I sat on the radiator inside, warming my skinny body.

    August had four sons, August Jr., Teddy, Henry, and Joey, and two daughters, Bertha and Jenny. August, the eldest son, and Bertha the eldest daughter, usually worked all night. I saw them in the wee hours of the morning running in and out of the oven room delivering fresh baked bread and a variety of sweets to the showcases. The other four siblings worked hard, too, early morning and after school. August, a widower, lived upstairs in his building with his six children, his deceased wife's sister, and her son, Eddie Preodor, who was a fellow classmate of mine and an outstanding professional violinist. (In his teens during the summer months, when the upstairs windows were wide open, I could hear Eddie practicing a block away at 4:30 in the morning.)

Mr. Bratulich, of Slovenian descent, was the kindest, most charitable gentleman. He always had many soft-spoken gems of wisdom for me. He was a wise counselor who helped direct high school and college activities. He served on the Eveleth School Board for many years as a dedicated community citizen. When he ran for election every few years, he never failed to receive far more votes than any of his fellow board members.

Many freezing winter and cold summer mornings, as I waited for my bus on his radiator, he would come in from the ovens to load up his bakery cases and see me soaking up his free heat. It was always a "Hi, Jovey," and "Hi, Mr. Bratulich." Then he'd slide open a display case, reach down and pick a freshly baked sweet and say, "Here, you must be hungry." (God, I was always hungry.)

Years later his eldest daughter, Bertha, married my second eldest brother, John, and his other daughter, Jennie, married my third eldest brother, Rudy. So, not only because of what I learned from him, but through marriage, he was forever a part of our family.

Treasure in The Ice

One of those cutting, below-zero mornings, I had just completed my newspaper route, which ended at Jackson Street. I was coming home on McKinley Avenue, only three blocks from home and a warm bed. On the corner was the Parlanti and Negri Grocery store, "our" grocery store, where we could charge everything and pay the bill when the mining check came in. I recall the exhilaration I felt when Mother allowed me to go pay the bill, because Mr. Parlanti or Mr. Negri always gave us a treat, generally a big five-cent candy bar.

On that early morning, about 6:30, I was crossing Garfield

Street with my head bent down to see the path, when I spied a slip of green sticking out of the frozen snow. I stopped, naturally: what grows green in fifty below? I bent down and suddenly saw it was a dollar bill, frozen. How could I dig it out without ruining it or getting run over? Fortunately, I always carried a Boy Scout knife in my newspaper bag. I knelt and started chipping at the ice on the well-lit street.

Now, Garfield Street was not all Catholic. On it lived Lutherans, Methodists and a scattering of Episcopalians, all getting ready to go to work in the mines. So when they opened their lace curtains and looked down and saw me in a kneeling position, they probably said, "There's that nutty Catholic Joey DeBevec, saying the rosary in the middle of the street and it's 50 degrees below zero."

I was really praying that I would get that dollar bill in one piece before I froze to death! After what seemed an eternity, I finally dug it out: a $10 bill! Equivalent to my salary for three weeks of peddling my heavy newspapers in bitter, frustrating, miserable, debilitating winter weather! My feet didn't touch the ground for the three blocks to my warm Summit Street home.

I crawled into bed for the two hours before school started and began wondering who had lost that bill? Someone, I figured, coming from Parlanti and Negri's grocery store who had just cashed their mining paycheck the night before, who had paid their bill and had ten dollars left until next month. I rationalized keeping the money by telling myself that it didn't have any owners' identification, and I fell asleep clutching my new-found prosperity in my hand.

The Rich

I have the greatest respect for anyone who earns wealth.

Our country and our culture provide many opportunities for success. But with success comes the responsibility to share our wealth with those less fortunate, and to respect the dignity of all people, regardless of their financial position in society. I learned at an early age that this is not always the case: there were people of power and influence who would disrespect you because you were poor.

Between the ages of five and seventeen, I had up to 110 customers on my newspaper route. I have already described the conditions I worked in. After an hour and a half of faithful delivery for seven days, collection day was Saturday. I spent most of the day going from door to door. I had the route that contained what everyone called "the millionaire block." It consisted of all the richest people in town — mine owners, lawyers, doctors, and store owners.

Now, we gave each customer a card with Saturday dates on it and a little pocket on the bottom for the fifteen cents a week for delivery of the weeks' papers. (My share was three-and-a-half cents.) The card was supposed to be placed outside the door with the money in an attached pocket. I would punch the date and pick out my money and leave without disturbing them.

You've already guessed it, haven't you? You're right: those cheap, uncharitable, no goodniks on "millionaire block" never, ever had the fifteen cents in the pocket. So I'd have to ring the bell. Invariably, the maid or the wife would open the door. I'd politely ask for fifteen cents, and she'd look at me like I was the scum of the earth and say, "I haven't any change, so go down to my husband's office and collect it."

Can you imagine? Untold riches and not fifteen cents in the house!

All the offices were downtown. So I had to go to the doctor's office and take my place in turn to see the doctor. There were sick patients ahead of me. When they finally called my name, I went in and he said, "What's wrong with you?"

I said, "I came to collect for a week of papers."

"Go collect it from my wife."

"I was there and she told me to come here."

Then he reached in his pocket. His hand came out with a fistful of bills, but no fifteen cents. He got out his prescription pad and wrote something. I said, "I'm feeling great. I don't need drugs, and anyhow, I'd rather have my fifteen cents."

He said, "Take this to the cashier."

The prescription read "Give him fifteen cents." I went to the cashier's office. There were quite a few ahead of me. I figured he owed a lot of people fifteen cents. I finally got paid.

The whole collection episode took two hours. I had the same problem with the two lawyers. The drug store owner was out for coffee. The mine owner was out inspecting his workers 1,200 feet under ground — that was a long wait! The engineer at the fee-owners' office was out somewhere engineering.

(P.S. These collection attempts actually occurred — honest! The collection episodes are slightly exaggerated.)

It was really frustrating because I broke my butt delivering their papers to earn three-and-a-half cents a week in weather ranging from 60 degrees above to 60 degrees below. Of 110 customers, I had ten of those ungrateful snobs. In addition, although the rich never even tipped me, I believed I had to give 115 percent to keep my job.

The other 100 of my customers were poor miners who worked to make the other ten rich. However, every one of those poor people had their little cards out with my 15 cents. The poor would watch for me, invite me in, insist I have a meal with them, offer me gifts to take home, like homemade bread, a ring of home-made sausage, a slice of poticia (a famous nut bread), a ring of blood sausage, a home knit scarf, a jar of pigs-feet jelly, pastries, a bottle of wine. This from Italians, Swedes, Norwegians, Turks, Slovenians, Serbians, Croatians, Finnish — all beautiful people, immigrants who built the greatest country anywhere.

Fortunately, the joy among the many "poor" in our community more than made up for my learning experiences with a few of the rich.

Strawberry Salesman

Some men can plant strawberries, some men can grow strawberries, but some men just do not know how to sell strawberries. In July 1930, one year after the stock market crash and the beginning of the Depression, everyone was out of work, or close to it. One sunny day, my close friend Schnoppa and I were sitting on a curb on Summit Street planning our next financial adventure when we saw a Model T Ford pickup truck with a long back stopping and starting as it moved up the street. A man walked from it to each house in the neighborhood with small baskets of something. But he came back to his truck each time with the baskets still full.

We approached him and noticed the open bed of his truck loaded with quart baskets of fresh strawberries — jillions of them — in a glistening red pyramid.

"You're not doing very well, are you?" we asked.

He said, "Well, I guess times are poor."

I said, "No, the times are really not that poor. Only your sales techniques for a small town are poor, and you're also in a poor section of a poor town. The ethnic population mistrusts anyone who lives more than a block away."

I continued, "Where are you from?"

He said, "Spooner, Wisconsin, about 80 miles from here."

I said, "You come that far to sell strawberries?"

He said, "Well, they keep growing and I have to keep picking and moving them."

"There are streets where the rich live and probably eat fresh fruit every day," we told him, "and we can sell them all for you."

The selling price was ten cents a quart or three quarts for a quarter. We decided our cut should be one-and-one-half cents per quart basket. I told the man to stay behind the wheel, that we would tell him where to go.

Now, everyone in town knew Schnoppa and me as honest entrepreneurs and smart sales boys. We ran in and out of homes like ants. We cleaned out his mountain of strawberries in about four hours. He was amazed, amused, and grateful. He gladly paid us off and said he would return in two days with another load. We told him to pile his truck higher and to attach a trailer because there were other towns nearby with strawberry potential.

He repeated his long trek from Spooner three more times, and each time all he hauled home was money and an empty truck bed. After emptying his truck the fourth time, he said he would like to show his appreciation by taking us back to his farm to see where our product was harvested and have us stay over one night with his wife and small children. We told our parents where we were going and that we would be back in two days. We had a marvelous time eating all the strawberries we could, drinking quarts of fresh milk, and consuming heaping plates of fresh farm food.

As luck would have it, during a tour nearby, we saw, to our amazement, the most important man in the U.S. at his vacation retreat: President Coolidge. We didn't get to shake his hand or to tell him we voted for him (we were only fifteen), but we did get to see him roaming around in his garden.

Giovannini

Shortly after Schnoppa and I very amicably parted ways, around 1932, I teamed up with Leo Giovannini. He was my age, a fellow student and a neighbor with whom I had an amiable relationship. His dad and mother had a corner grocery store right across the street from our home. At seventeen, we were handsome, aggressive, good speakers and good dancers, which was very important in Eveleth — sometimes more so than having a good education.

One day after I had completed some financial adventure, Leo and I were discussing how we could augment our income. I reminded him that a circus was coming into town. He said in his stentorian, legal voice, "It may be a rumor, so we should verify it."

Silence. Leo talked like a lawyer from the time he was twelve; he eventually became a successful lawyer.

Then I said, "And they always charge a helluva lot for gum, candy, and ice cream."

He said, "Indubitably!"

Silence. "Well," I said, "why don't we set up our own booth next to the circus. We'll put in a lot of goodies and cut the hell out of prices and still make a bundle."

He agreed, but as we had little money, I suggested we order what we needed from the wholesaler his father used and put it on the Giovannini tab. Then, when we had enough to pay the bills, we would pay him and order more.

Leo said, "Perhaps our food venture will collapse because of inclement weather."

No "silence" this time. I bellowed, "Leo, stop that legal bull-crap chatter and listen to me. You can't win without taking a chance — capisch?" When you spoke Italian to Leo, he shut up.

Now we had to build a booth and erect shelves out of old

boards and used canvas we found in our yards. We collected it all, piled it on a wagon, and hauled it up to the circus site, an empty lot between Ben Franklin School and the ball park. Near the entrance to the circus, we started to build our makeshift booth.

We got two boards nailed and out stormed a red-faced circus employee who screamed, "What the hell are you doing?"

With legal decorum, Leo replied, "We're building an ice cream and candy booth to please our fellow Evelethians."

He yelled, "You can't!"

I said, "It's city property."

He said, "Just a minute. I'll be back." He returned with the circus owner and his legal counsel. Hell, I didn't worry. I just sent Leo, my high school lawyer against them. But then a police officer came along and a brouhaha developed and poor Leo lost. They claimed we were encroaching (I didn't know what that was, but Leo did) on rental property. The police officer warned us that we could not erect our stand on any spot from the sidewalk to the street. We pleaded that we could not build it on the sidewalk. He said we could build it on the street. We pointed out the danger of that and that we would congest it. We asked, "How about the six-foot grass boulevard between the street and the sidewalk?" He winked and said, "Go ahead, but don't tell anyone I gave you permission." He was the nicest guy. I'm sure he was Italian.

We hastily put up two-by-fours for corner posts, a large piece of worn canvas for the roof, and rudely constructed shelves. We had decided to offer only best sellers: Cracker Jack, boxes of popcorn, ice cream cones, candy bars, Wrigley chewing gum, and Eskimo pies.

I sent Leo to canvass the concession stands run by the circus personnel to check their prices. He reported that they were offering the items that we intended to stock at ten cents. We could cut our price to five cents and still make money. We had no expensive corporate heads, no salaries, no overhead expenses, no electricity, no worker wages, no advertising, no taxes, no janitor, no union fees, no legal fees (Leo worked free) — what a business!

The circus opened with all its hoopla Sunday at noon and stayed open noon to midnight through the following Saturday. After Leo and I attended early mass on Sunday, we went to our establishment. The truck came with all our products (we had ordered them the day before) and we were ready for our grand opening. However, we never anticipated the avalanche of customers. We were busier than two one-armed paper hangers. Ice cream came in tall 10-inch diameter steel tubes three feet tall, inside rock ice insulated by four-foot tall thick canvas cases. It would keep hard for days. We had three flavors, vanilla, chocolate, and strawberry. And we served generous scoops for only a nickel a cone. Our boxes of gum, Cracker Jack, popcorn, and candy bars emptied like water running through a sieve.

We had planned for a successful operation and we knew we would need fresh supplies quickly, so we had asked a family across the street to borrow their phone for emergency reordering. We worked from early morning to midnight every day for seven days, a constant filling of shelves, hustling sales, reordering stock, refilling stock, telephoning, and emptying the booth completely at midnight, to haul what was left home in small wagons. It was dark by 5:00 p.m., minutes before our rush hour, but since we were on the corner of a street, the city furnished street light without charge. But we still had to conduct our service and transactions with the aid of flashlights. With flashlight in one hand and an ice cream or sweet in the other, we had quite a juggling act to transact the exchange of money. But the operation was a terrific experience, and very profitable. We didn't make enough to send Leo to law school — but it helped!

Our Musical Heritage

Dad played the button accordion, a beautiful German Hohner. My eldest brother Tony learned it from Dad and later advanced to a piano accordion. He became an excellent accordionist. He played everywhere and earned a lot of money. He taught all five brothers to play both button and piano accordions. We all picked up the accordion during our few leisure moments. Tony and Frankie became professionals, but we four just played for our own amusement.

Tony envisioned a future family orchestra. He had five brothers and a sister with a heaven-sent voice, so his dream eventually came true. I was twelve years old when he decided I should play an instrument other than the button and piano accordion, which he played well and I poorly. My mother and father didn't decide — he did, as the eldest son. The violin was sissy stuff to me, but I played it, just as Tony decreed and eventually played it very well.

Tony bought me my first fiddle. Then he looked for someone who gave private lessons. He couldn't find anyone locally. He heard of a violin teacher in nearby Hibbing and he prayed that this guy would come to Eveleth to teach the violin. I was praying he wouldn't. My brother won.

Families all over town conspired to bring this exalted teacher to our town. A tall, skinny, bald-headed man of German descent, he probably worked in the Hibbing mines and taught violin on his days off. But he was good. He was kind, thoughtful, and patient. He never hit students with his baton; however, he would rap it very hard on the music stand.

Once a week on Saturday, probably his day off, I would take my violin under my arm in a washed-out Universal cement sack, which served as my case. (Mother once sewed nine of these sacks together for sheets and that's what we slept on for many years.) I would then walk about nine blocks to the basement of the Italian hall where we would-be violin virtuosos showed "his eminence" how much we had progressed in one week.

The charge per lesson was twenty-five cents (a lot of money in 1927), and Tony paid it. Sometimes, when we were low on cash, I would bring a ring of Slovenian sausage that Dad made. When I opened the bag to bargain with him for my fee, he always succumbed.

I practiced hard. I drove our family crazy every day practicing on that screechy three-dollar violin. I never gave up. I eventually purchased an expensive violin with longtime savings. My beloved high school violin teacher, Nicolas Furjanic, had bought it in Prague, Czechoslovakia where he practiced and taught every summer. I also learned to play the bass and eventually made extra income to augment my meager salary as a sales associate at the J.C. Penney store. I played for small groups, our family orchestra, the Martin Shukel Orchestra, the Virginia Symphony, and the Hibbing Symphony.

The time came when I faced a lifetime opportunity and I had to make a major career decision: I was asked to audition for the Duluth Symphony under the direction of Paul LeMay. He had heard me play at one of my gigs and Mr. Furjanic recommended me. At that time the Duluth Symphony was well regarded. I auditioned and was accepted. I was exhilarated beyond my wildest dreams.

The orchestra practiced every Wednesday at 7:00 p.m. and played a concert every Sunday at 1:00 p.m. The pay was ten dollars for each concert. My exuberance, however, was quickly diminished. I was working full-time as Assistant Manager at the J.C. Penney store in Eveleth for $40 a month. I was their top sales person every month. Duluth was 60 miles away. We didn't work on

Sunday afternoon so that was no problem. But the Penney store closed at 6:00 and I always had to stay late to straighten up the store. I could never make it in time to the rehearsal at 7 pm each Wednesday.

I explained my problem to my store manager, Hilding Erick Carlson. I asked if he would allow me to leave forty-five minutes earlier than usual every Wednesday so I could fulfill a lifetime ambition. He didn't know that I worked 12 hours a day, six days, and many nights when the store was closed, and got paid for only forty-eight hours. He listened to my plea and asked very gently, "When does your first practice begin?"

I said, "This Wednesday."

He said, "You have my permission."

I was almost speechless. I blurted out "I have!"

He said, "Yes, you have. You may leave at 5:15 this Wednesday, but don't ever come back!"

I didn't go. I stayed with Penney's and Mr. Carlson for four years and came to respect and love him. He became a great friend, and an excellent teacher. He watched me progress in various stores with complete admiration and pride. I stayed with the J.C. Penney Co. for thirty-nine years in nine different stores in three states and managed three different stores. And every transfer was a promotion. I was successful at Penney's beyond my wildest dreams.

But I have always wondered what happened to the string bass player who took my place.

J.C. Penney

I started working for the J.C. Penney Company at 1:00 p.m. on May 9, 1936, a Saturday. I was attending Eveleth Junior College for the third year at the time. School was over, but I was doing some odd jobs — I had more odd jobs than Heinz has varieties. I had walked to town and was crossing the town square on Main Street, on my way to buy a pack of cigarettes at the Red Owl store.

I met a man crossing the street opposite me. We stopped in the middle of the square in the middle of Main Street and stood there face-to-face on a steel manhole cover. There were not many cars in those days so we didn't flinch or budge. He had a bank bag in his hand and was going to make a deposit at the First National Bank on the corner. He said to me, "Go home and put a tie on and come to work at 1:00." That's all he said.

Now, I knew only that the man, Mr. Carlson, managed Penney's, but apparently he knew a helluva lot about me. Everybody in town did. I bustled with energy and enthusiasm and was involved in everything. My response was "Yes, sir!" That's all I said. After this short conversation, I left to get my Lucky Strikes and he to unload his cash at the bank.

Coming out of the Red Owl store, I suddenly realized I had only forty-five minutes to jog to our home on St. Mary's Lake, a ten-mile round trip, get a tie, and be back in time for work. I was speedy, but that was impossible. So I jogged a mile to my sister Aggie's home, dashed in, grabbed a tie off her husband's rack, and dashed out. Fortunately I had a decent dress shirt on and a pair of acceptable dress pants that I had put on to work at school.

I worked at Penney's that day from 1:00 p.m. to closing time at 6:00 p.m. and then straightened up for another hour. In those six hours I never asked Mr. Carlson what pay I was to receive or the longevity of my position. After asking the assistant manager the store hours I went home.

The next day was Sunday. The store was closed, but I found out the store opened Monday morning at 8:00 when the manager came. But the assistant manager always came at 7:00

a.m., so I was there filling shelves and sweeping the floor at 7:00 a.m. In came Mr. Carlson, the manager. He said, "What the hell are you doing here? I didn't tell you to come back."

And I said as pleasantly as I could, "Mr. Carlson, you didn't tell me not to come back."

He said, "Well, I'll be damned!" and grinned and went up to his office.

I stayed with J.C. Penney for thirty-nine years!

I worked for Mr. Carlson from 7:00 a.m. to 7:00 p.m. Monday through Friday, and Saturday 7:00 a.m. to 10:00 p.m. On Sundays and many nights we worked with no pay to dress windows, fill stock, oil the wood floor, order merchandise, paint signs, decorate the interior, and take inventory. We were not allowed to leave until Mr. Carlson approved each department. I remember one night (in a hurry to go to a dance at the "rec"), I hurried the pants' piles. He insisted all folds be in line and piled neatly in perfect unison, and they weren't. He took his two large hands and swept all of the pants off the table onto the floor and said, not quietly, "Do them over and do them right."

My pay was seven-and-a-half cents an hour. I was laughed at and ridiculed by some of my friends and young men my age who went to work in the mines. They came into the store to cash their paychecks and would flaunt them, saying, "Joey, look what I get. $120 a month, while you make $40 a month working for this cheap company." And they stayed where they were and died there — early. And I left and saw the world, advanced beyond my expectations, and made a lot of money for the company and myself. I transferred, with a promotion each time, to five stores as Assistant Manager and three stores as Manager, in three different states over thirty-nine years.

The J.C. Penney Company was one of the first corporations in America to establish a profit-sharing plan for everyone from the manager to the janitor. It was also the first to create a medical plan and a dental plan — long before the unions, mines, schools, and governments ever enacted them. And the Penney Company assumed 95 percent of the expense.

In 1948, after the Board of Directors chose me, I attended a J.C. Penney national convention in Chicago where I received my HSCC pin (Honor, Service, Confidence, Cooperation) as an official manager. Mr. Penney personally "pinned" me and then he handed me a card that would be the foundation on which I would conduct myself in and out of business for the rest of my life. The "rule" it carried was adopted in 1913 — they called it the "Penney Idea" and it is just as good for me today and will be for time eternal.

The company issued a confidential book for managers only, called "The Red Book." Its cover carried the warning: "This book must never be permitted to leave the office or store." It was an operational manual on every action necessary to manage the store profitably. It contained nothing illegal or dishonest; it was a book of rules based on the integrity that Mr. Penney set down for his company, which never cheated either its customers or associates since 1902. (All Penney personnel are called associates.)

To be a manager, I needed to learn these rules. So, very secretly, I would go down to the store at night. Mr. Carlson would rarely be there and I would get out the Red Book and study until I had memorized it all.

My problem was that in the town of Eveleth, the police officer on night duty came on their rounds to check every business door on Main Street every night to be sure it was locked. So I would ask who was on duty and notify him that I would be up in the office in the back of the store, which he could see. When he rattled the door, I would get up from the desk in the office so he could see me. He would wave, I would wave and he would move on, and I kept burning the midnight oil. Mr. Penney never knew this, but he certainly expected this kind of loyalty from his associates. It paid off.

The Penney Idea

I was always happy to be a J.C. Penney manager because, throughout the history of our beloved company, part of our company policy has always been to think in terms of debt to the community. We encourage all our associates to take an active interest in the community, for we recognize that the privileges of private initiative are not without their public responsibilities and obligations. We don't conceive of our partnership as limited to the associates who receive part of their compensation from our profits, but as one between every store and its community, with both the company and the community profiting by every transaction.

I started employment with J.C. Penney on May 9, 1936 and retired June 1, 1975, a continuous, loyal labor of love for thirty-nine years. And never, not once, was I absent from daily work for any reason — sickness, injury, or operations! For thirty-nine years!

I could not afford to be absent because I wanted to continue as top salesperson of the store every month. Since the individual sales figures were reported monthly to the district office, zone office, and New York headquarters, I felt that someone in the higher echelons of the Penney Company was bound to take notice of the sales records of poor skinny Joey DeBevec in a small store in a small town. And they did. That is the way to get promotions. And I did. I was transferred five times to assistant managership and three times to store manager in different states in only twenty years.

<u>The Penney Idea, adopted 1913</u>
To serve the public, as nearly as we can, to its
complete satisfaction.
To expect for the service we render a fair remuneration
and not all the profit the traffic will bear.
To do all in our power to pack the customer's dollar full
of value and not all the profit the traffic will bear.
To continue to train ourselves and our associates so that the
service we give will be more and more intelligently performed.
To improve constantly the human factor in business.
To reward men and women in our organization through
participation in what the business produces.
To test our every policy, method and act in this wise:
"Does it square with what is right and just?"

Many people told me I stopped too soon at the store-manager level in the Penney Co. They said I could have gone all the way to the top: District Manager, Zone Manager, maybe to the corporate level. I had the carriage, brains, composure, personality, good looks, ability to govern, and penchant for organizing. And I loved people.

But I lacked one important thing: I did not want to pay the penalty. I had to decide where ambition ends and fulfillment of life begins. And going to the top would mean I would lose my most precious asset — time with my family. I watched sympathetically as many of my superiors, because of their continual absences from their families, got out of touch with them.

Life has to be more than years spent on self-indulgence, career advancements, monetary gains, and work. What really counts is a united family. Everything else is secondary. Keeping a family together is no easy task. It is the absolute toughest job we have to face because every other influence is out to destroy the family unit.

You can't let your job or profession turn into a labor camp. Hard work is essential, but there must be time for rest and relaxation, for going to see your child in a school play or a swim meet. If you don't do these things while the children are young, there is no way to make it up later. If you conquer the world and your children turn out badly, you will have to consider yourself a complete failure. By the time they reach twenty-one, all their habits are molded — good or bad.

Krazy Daze

In the retail business, mid-summer is a transition period. Summer items are at the end of their cycle and back-to-school sales have not yet begun. It's the doldrums for a small businessman who is trying to clear out any overstocked items for fall merchandise and keep his cash flow flowing. In 1956, I discovered a terrific way to beat the sales slump and helped establish a retail tradition that spread all over Minnesota and neighboring states.

We lived in Morris at the time, a small farming community in the flat western regions of Minnesota. On our way home from a family vacation, I witnessed a wild street sale going on in a Wisconsin town. Usually I avoided doing anything related to business on family trips, but this scene was remarkable enough to stop me in my tracks. Customers were flocking to tables set out in fronts of stores loaded with clearance items. It was a feeding frenzy.

When we got back to Morris, I tried to persuade other business owners to have our own outdoor, mid-summer sale. They thought I was out of my mind! No one else in the business community joined me, so I decided I'd go it alone. I placed several newspaper ads to announce "Krazy Daze" at Penney's. I borrowed $50 for change from a business friend for a cigar box cash register, got some silly clothes, put merchandise on bales of hay and sold bottles of Coke for a nickel. By 10:00 am I had sold everything, including the bales of straw. I had done more business in two hours than I had done on any day of the year prior. It was a sensational promotion. Next year everyone was there and within a few years it had spread like wildfire through the state as a way to clear out the late summer doldrums.

Last Nail

Gary Cummings, a great Assistant Manager of mine at J.C. Penney in Little Falls, Minnesota surprised me with a telephone call, years after I retired. In our conversation, he reminded me of a gem of wisdom I had imparted to him as I trained him. To ensure that our customers were treated with utmost respect and served to their satisfaction, I often placed myself at the entrance to my store to thank them for their business. Once I noticed a young boy wearing new shoes, but who was limping. I asked him what was wrong. He said, "I just bought a new pair of shoes from that big tall guy and they hurt, but I suppose new shoes are supposed to hurt."

I sat him down on a nearby chair and examined his shoes. A sharp nail was sticking through the heel into the shoe. Shoe manufacturers in those days attached the upper shoe to the sole before stitching with a "last nail." Generally they would remove it at the factory, but not always. So I took the boy back and confronted Gary, who had sold the boy his shoes. "When you sell a pair of shoes, the Penney Company procedure is to check every shoe for a 'last nail.' Either file it off so it won't hurt or get a pair of damn pliers and yank the thing out!" I don't think he ever missed the last nail again, and he sold a lot of shoes in his career.

Success

As the poor son of a poor miner, ever since childhood, I told myself, "There must be more to life than this. There must be a better way!" I didn't want to work in the mines like my five brothers, or end up like anyone else I knew. I wanted to be a leader, not a follower, because leaders, no matter how materially poor, get to use all of their talents and are the ones who influence others. But I realized that, to compete against those whose parents gave them everything, I would really have to bust my butt and gut to outwork and outproduce them. And apparently I did.

I had to be stronger than they were mentally, morally, spiritually, and physically. Strength does not come from winning. You can fail and lose many times, but in struggling to win after loss, you develop strengths that amaze even yourself. I knew I had to go through many more hardships than my young rich friends and competitors, and to decide never to quit. That is strength! You have to decide to be numero uno. You have to be hungry for success — not over others, but through others.

Baseball — A Game of Failure

People pay $25 to $1000 to attend a baseball game to see an endless parade of failures. The batters have an average of something between zero and 400; only two batters in history had over 400 (Ted Williams had a 406). Perhaps only 10 percent of all players bat 300 for a season. That means that during a full season a player goes to the plate ten times and fails to get a hit seven times. And for such a poor performance he gets to be a world hero — is mobbed and idolized by fans. And he gets paid two to three million dollars a season, and millions for endorsing products that he never buys or uses. Can you imagine any other field of endeavor that idolizes and pays that well? Doctors failing seven of ten operations? Dentists failing seven of ten fillings? Plumbers failing seven of ten repairs? Factory workers failing to produce a good product seven times out of ten? Teachers failing seven out of ten students? Police failing in seven out of ten arrests? An auto mechanic failing in seven out of ten motor repairs?

And the baseball players are having the time of their lives running around a manicured, green velvet sea of clipped grass, 164 games a year for only three hours a game. Everyone else, except other athletes, has to play 261 to 313, eight-to-ten hour "games" a year — in much more important jobs. And with no respect, no adulation, and nothing like the pay!

Something to think about.

You Can Do Anything

As a young man I was a workaholic. I was never still. I never just sat around and wasted time, when I knew of so many interesting things and projects to explore. You can't win any personal battles being a couch potato, and I was a perfectionist and super-aggressive. But I was still loving. I loved life and loved people. I hated no one — I just wanted to beat my competitors fair and square in any endeavor.

I couldn't lose. What would I lose with that kind of philosophy, which costs nothing? You can't buy it anywhere. You build it yourself. In the end, I could accept both successes and failures. I was always willing to try again to right any error I made and to have good feelings about myself whether in success or failure. Furthermore, I was extremely confident, had great self-discipline, self image, and self-esteem. I thought I could just about do anything.

At dinner in August of 1993 at the home of our daughter's

close friends in Kingston, Ontario, the host, Clyde Negus, who doesn't profess either to look or act like a philosopher, came out with this dandy: "It's no shame to be poor or ignorant, but it's a damn shame to stay that way."

Family Stories

For love, not money

My DAD, WHOM I WORSHIPED, had a lousy, poorly paid job mining iron ore. The mines were always on strike and he had seven hungry mouths to feed. And of course, he would die before he accepted welfare, which none of us ever did. He did me the great favor of being an example of frugality and discipline. Because all he had to give me was his love, I praise him forever for never:

> Giving me a penny.
> Financing my education.
> Buying me an ice cream cone.
> Helping build me a home.
> Buying me a car.
> Buying me a violin.
> Buying me a string bass.
> Painting my house.
> Paying my mortgage.
> Paying my hospital bills.

You see, he forced me to earn and learn to do it myself — and I did, beyond either of our wildest dreams.

On one of my rare visits to my hometown in their later years, I went to see my father and mother. He was at his job as a janitor at the city-owned auditorium in Eveleth (working in those back-breaking mines had taken its toll; this job was something he could handle in his late years). I was anxious to see him so I went to the auditorium. I entered the front door and in a little side office found the boss of the working crew. I said, "I want to see Tony DeBevec." I was not being disrespectful, but the boss got up and gave me a hard look and said, "Who are you?"

I said, "I'm Joey, his son."

And he reddened and said, "Don't you ever come in this place again and ask for 'Tony.' You say, 'I want to see my father. Understand?'"

There I was, a successful Penney manager, making three times a month more than he and my father collectively. I said, "I'm sorry. Yes, sir."

He smiled and said, "He's in the kitchen mopping the floor."

Now there was a man! I admired Paul Cesaretti and I never forgot his admonition. On future visits, he always had a warm welcome and smile and kind words for me.

Bud Mack

Bud Mack was my first wife's grandfather. He called her "Dorsey" (Dorothy) and in his prime could out-drink anyone in town. But when we came to visit him before and after our marriage, he always insisted on our joining him in a cup of tea!

Grandpa Mack had been a lumberjack. His wife had died and he lived alone in a small house in Virginia, Minnesota, which had once been a lumberjack mecca where millions of logs floated down to Virginia saw mills.

He was a five-foot three-inch Irishman who sired five huge lumberjack sons, each more than six feet tall — big, strong, fighting specimens from such a diminutive father. When his wife, who had been six inches taller than he, died, the sons scattered to all points of the earth. But he remained in his little house.

Every day at eighty years of age, he'd arise early and have his pot of tea and toast and then, with much deliberation, he would get dressed as if he were going to some regal affair. His upper eyelids drooped with age, which interfered with his vision, and his unusually long eyelashes continually got into his eye, causing his tear ducts to erupt. So, once he was dressed, he would meticulously tape his upper lashes and eyelids to his eyebrows.

Now, all dressed up in his Sunday best and with his eyes looking like something from outer space, he would pull himself up to his full, if diminutive, height, square his shoulders, and go forth to battle, walking about twelve blocks to his favorite pub downtown. There, he shuffled through the sawdust, climbed up on a chair (they were high in those days), placed his feet on the bar rail (it took a bit of stretching), and before he had time to sigh, had a drink in front of him. After years of this, the bartender knew he wanted a "Boilermaker" — a double whiskey shot chased down with a mug of beer.

It didn't take many of those before he got belligerent — which was his intent. So in due time he was ready to assert his physical prowess against anyone at the bar. All of the patrons knew him, so they all played along, letting him punch while they held him by his vest at arms' length. Rarely, his punches fell on his adversaries, like puffs of cotton or errant confetti.

Finally the bartender would announce, "Time, gentlemen, please!" It was only noon. The other patrons knew the bar would be open for many more hours, but Grandpa would say, "Glory be to God, have I been here that long?" The bartender would then pick up the earphone from the wall telephone and shout a number into the mouthpiece and within five minutes a police car would arrive. The officer would approach Grandpa and say, "Well, Bud, how did ya do today?" and Grandpa would reply, "Well, I got two but one got away." Then the police officer would guide or half-carry him to the police car, stuff him in, drive him to his home, guide him to the back door (front door was only for company), and help him in. "OK, Bud, get into bed," the police officer would tell him, and as he closed the door, the officer would hear the raw, strained voice of this Irish leprechaun scratching out, "Toorah Loorah Loorah Toorah Loorahlie."

Dorothy Mack

I met my wife Dorothy at a Saturday night dance at the Eveleth "Rec." I loved to dance all my life so it was fitting that I would meet my wife on the dance floor.

The Rec was the biggest building in town with a huge wood-floored presentation area, perfect for dancing. It became the center of entertainment every Saturday night. None of us went with dates. You always went with your friends. Girls with girls, guys with guys. People also sat in the bleachers around the dance floor and just listened and watched.

My buddies and I would get a half pint of bourbon (to share between all of us) and head over to a cafe where we would drink, brag, and prepare for the evening. I remember walking into the Rec and spying Dorothy for the first time. I knew she wasn't from Eveleth, she came over from nearby Virginia. She really stood out because she was tall, beautiful, and had a graceful carriage. My first words to her were "Doge noge!" (pronounced (dogah nogah), which is Slovenian for "long legs!" We spent the night dancing together. She must've been impressed because less than a year later, I was married to the most elegant, beautiful lady on the range, Dorothy Ann Mack. We enjoyed dancing throughout our lives.

Jeff's Birth

Our firstborn son Jeff was born in 1947 in Iron Mountain, Michigan where I was Assistant Manager of the J.C. Penney store. Two of my closest friends were Dr. Raemer Smith, our family doctor and the one who delivered Jeff, and Ernest Brown, the prosecuting attorney of Dickinson County.

Jeff's mother was in the delivery room but either false starts or a faulty warning system were not yet producing our first child. I remember holding onto my wife's arms and hands and helping her push. Finally, they brought in a tray of food for her. She was, understandably, not interested so I sat there and ate the whole thing. Suddenly, I saw that black-haired head and Jeff made his grand entrance. I watched the whole delivery, which was rare in those days, along with his first embrace with his mother.

I said, "Doc Raemer, we have to celebrate."

He said, "Great! Let me wash up."

I said, "I'll go and pick up Ernie across the street and the three of us will go up to my house to begin the fireworks." I had saved some bottles of German brandy and French champagne for this occasion. I had them shipped home from Germany after World War II in a big crate labeled "military books."

We drank our favorite drink from overseas —two shots of brandy poured into a glass of champagne. We called it a "French 75" after a powerful French artillery piece. After consuming an abnormal amount of this potent concoction, we visited our favorite watering holes in the surrounding towns — all of them! At 5:00 a.m., my two comrades were in no condition to be taken to their homes, so I brought them to mine and bedded them down. None of us went to work the next day.

This caused a flurry of telephone calls and ad hoc search parties. My two devoted friends were pillars of society, and they had not gone to bed in their own homes. They finally found the doctor's car in front of my home and came in and found us alive, but not well. But Jeff was alive and well, thanks to God, and although he was only twelve hours old, he was thoroughly toasted by the best of men and spirits.

Before Jeff's baptismal day, I went to Monsignor Pelissier at St. Mary's Church to make the arrangements. Father was not only a cherished friend, but a confidante and personal spiritual adviser. He asked what we wanted to name him. I said, "I've always liked the name 'Jeff,' so let's name him Jeffrey, and I want him to have his mother's name, which was Mack."

Father gently replied, "Joseph, the Church does not permit any names but those of saints. I will have to give this some prayerful thought." I thought nothing more of it. On baptismal day, we came to the font with our dear friends, Jerry and Mary Miller, as godparents. Monsignor Pelissier dipped the child, intoning, "I baptize thee in the name of the Father and of the Son and of the Holy Ghost Jeffrey Mack Joseph Michael." That son of a gun got the "saints to come marching in."

Raising Kids

How I laugh at the punishments meted out by today's parents. The parents of a child who has done something wrong, even if they are thoroughly shocked at the behavior, shout, "Go to your room and don't come out until you say you're sorry." The child hides a smirk on his face, secretly murmuring, "My room — great!" Nothing could please him more because he has $4,000 worth of modern toys there. After an hour he gets bored, so he opens the door and sings, "I'm sorry!" "Well, that's just fine — now you can come out."

This is ridiculous! In my day parents were trying to raise children to respect their moral obligations. Their discipline and their punishment were severe. They wanted what they doled out to change us — for the good. In the one-room shack I was born in, my parents found it impossible to banish us to our room. And later, in a six-room house with seven kids, we slept three to a room — in one bed! If they sent us to our rooms, three bored kids without toys would be at each others' throats. There was no TV to forbid (today that punishment would cause a child to think of committing suicide). So my mother made us kneel on firewood blocks stacked in a pyramid for one hour in separate areas of the kitchen where she could watch us. Now that's what I call punishment. I never had to be punished like that twice.

I can just see the shock of today's parents reading this. Bull, I say! My mother and father lived to be eighty-nine and eighty-five. We loved and respected them all their lives. They raised seven children with very few material assets. Not one of us left home until we were in our early twenties. Not one of us ever:

Questioned their authority.

Disobeyed them.

Talked back to them.

Swore at them.

Cheated them.

Took drugs.

Got any girl pregnant before marriage.

Drank to excess.

Stole.

Murdered.

Raped.

Went to jail.

Had a car wreck.

Caused them any financial problems.

Asked for money.

Took money from them for education or any other reason.

Embarrassed them.

Shirked the work they doled out.

That's a pretty good track record, because all of us lived into our seventies and eighties. We were great kids! Great Americans! Some things change, but not this: proper discipline results in proper respect, which results in proper conduct. And that should never change.

The Piano

In 1955, we lived in Morris, Minnesota where I managed a J.C. Penney store. Mike was five years old and Jeff was nine. Both were students at the Catholic grade school run by nuns, the pillars who maintain the excellence of Catholic schools.

I never owned a piano, but I played from the age of fourteen. I wanted a piano for our sons but I just couldn't swing the purchase at that time. The nuns had a beautiful grand piano and gave lessons for a small fee. So Mike and Jeff enrolled. They practiced after school and had their recitals on the grand piano in the convent. Under their strict supervision, they advanced admirably. I never worried about their progress. The good sisters never tolerated mediocrity, and the kids were twice-blessed because they got moral guidance with the lessons.

In 1960, I was transferred to Little Falls, Minnesota, as manager of the J.C. Penney store there. I was determined to buy a piano for the boys. I decided I would borrow money from the bank.

There was no piano store in any town within a fifty-mile

radius, so we had to have one shipped up from the Schmidt Music store in Minneapolis, a hundred miles away. The delivery men came to my home in the early afternoon on the next day. I was at the store when my wife called to say they had arrived. I ran home, three blocks away, climbed onto the truck parked in front of our home, and played all three models inside the truck. I said, "I'll take the tan Baldwin Acrosonic. It sounds the best." They wheeled it into our home, I gave them a check, and I ran three blocks back to work in my store.

The first item on our family musical agenda was to arrange for a music teacher. We found a saint, Sister Alicia Pischke of the order of Saint Francis in Little Falls. She taught the boys flair and finesse at the piano later when they entered nearby St. John's Preparatory School. Sister Alicia was an energetic teacher who produced positive results in all her students. Our sons and I still owe her a great debt of gratitude. She played an integral role in our family and we have remained friends and correspondents all our lives.

Then I had to figure out how to get the boys to practice. I decided the best way was to lure them by example. So I played the piano every day in their hearing to encourage them. It didn't take much. Both boys already had the calling and soon, getting them off the piano to come to dinner was hard. Those two wild kids would even fight each other to be the first to the piano after school to practice. Can you imagine having the honor of settling such a dispute? So I watched them after dinner every night, sitting in my chair with my feet up, my eyes closed, occasionally offering a comment or suggestion (more like a command, I'm sure) to improve their performances.

My wife, Dorothy, provided the biggest surprise. She couldn't carry a note if her life depended on it, but she secretly went down to Lovdahl's drug store and purchased a book titled

"How to Play the Piano Expertly in Three Weeks." And every day when the kids were in school and I was at the store, she practiced to keep music alive in our home. She followed the music sheets very well. I was amazed.

Sister Alicia had a yearly piano recital so her students could display their talents. She gave each student a special composition to play according to each one's ability. Sometimes, students got more than they could handle, or so it seemed. Sister Alicia, I'm sure, was providing a challenge for students she thought could meet the muster and master the music.

Mike came home one day with his piece to play at the recital. It was "Rondo Capricioso" by Mendelssohn, heady stuff to give to a twelve-year-old. Mike was too young to laugh and I was too old to cry at this unexpected trial. I encouraged him and promised to help him by listening to his nightly practice sessions.

The practicing went on for many weeks. Mike worked his heart out trying to please Sister Alicia and me. He had to face her at least once a week and me every day.

He finally said he was ready. The recital was held at the convent's high school auditorium. Many students of various piano teachers jammed the auditorium with their brothers, sisters, relatives, mothers, and fathers.

The younger children went on first. Finally it was time for our Mike to play.

He was always (and still is) an inveterate showman. He approached the seat, pulled it out, flipped the coattails of his suit over the back of the seat, and sat down. He paused for a moment to focus his thoughts on the music, then attacked the piano like a professional. This is a very fast and difficult piece that requires a lot of dexterity. And it's long. He played without music; he had learned it all by heart. He finished with a flourish of long glissandos to a standing ovation. Mother and I couldn't have been more proud.

Letter From Mike

December 25, 1973

Mom and Dad —

 Many changes occurred in my life during the past year. Superficially, at least. Marriage. Medical school. This is a thank-you letter for your role in my life during the past year, as well as during my entire life. Perhaps this is overdue, and so you say, "Aha! At last we worthy parents receive our payoff for our years of sacrifice." And here it is. I think that often you consider me to be ungrateful, but that is merely a result of your misunderstanding of me. I very much appreciate many things that you do for me, but I don't express my gratitude in the ways to which you are most accustomed. Moreover, the things that are important to you are not necessarily of the same degree of importance to me, which amazes you, and more often disappoints or saddens you. Perhaps the most frequent favors you do for me are financial — lending me money, helping me out when things are tight, etc. And for these favors, I thank you very much. I do appreciate your generosity, to me and to others. But I thank you even more for your behavior during the most difficult and trying months of my life — the months after I broke up with Annie. Despite the fact that I was living with you every day during that time, you didn't interfere, and yet I knew you were concerned. And you welcomed Annie back with open arms, without resentment, when we decided to get married. For these things, then, I thank you too.

 Lastly, I want to thank you most for something that you yourselves probably take for granted. It is probably your single most important contribution determining directly or indirectly the degree of happiness and satisfaction in my life. From my day of birth throughout my life, I have had parents who are happy with themselves, with each other, with their marriage, and with life.

This is the greatest gift you have given me — as great as life itself. I pray that I too can give it to my children, and I thank God that I have had parents that love each other and life as much as you do.

Love, Mike

Blessings

Salvation Army

$\mathbf{F}$ROM 1950 TO 1975 I WAS AN UNPAID committee-of-one who served as head of a Salvation Army extension unit that covered a county area. I dispensed funds for food, lodging, gas, and miscellaneous needs to a daily parade of transients, poor, out-of-luck, and stranded people, as well as those who came into the store for assistance in emergencies like fires and floods. I often organized Salvation Army sandwich and coffee trucks to come to my aid. I merely picked up the phone and called headquarters in Minneapolis, Minnesota, a hundred miles away, and their trucks, always on standby, fully equipped, would be in my city within a few hours.

I was on call twenty-four hours a day. Men who were "flippin freights" though Little Falls would come to my Penney store for help. Once a man needed shoes and showed me a scrap of paper that had my "code" name written on it: "Little Falls, J.C. Penney, Big Daddy." Any transient needing help, even at three in the morning needed only to go to the police station, find out where I lived, and come knocking at my door at home. This wasn't a daily or nightly occurrence, but it happened often enough to make my first wife, Dorothy, understandably jittery.

I also had to raise the money to help those who came to my area for assistance and to pay for the supplies that came by truck for emergencies. The fund-raising was really not that time-consuming. I never left the store to do it. Gracious people who heard of my work brought in generous checks unsolicited. Each year I'd call headquarters in Minneapolis to send my saint — Major Carlson, a single, middle-aged former carpenter, with an unforgettable thick Swedish accent — to come up in full uniform to pick up their donations. He also went on his own private calls and canvassed every store on Main Street. Before his visit, I contacted newspaper and radio stations that were generous with free publicity. Everyone was so kind and gentle and generous to him.

I knew Major Carlson for twenty-five years and I called on him every year to come to any town or city where I was managing a J.C. Penney store. He would come from Minneapolis by bus, though he often hitchhiked. He traveled in uniform with nothing but a Bible and a well-used leather strapped black brief case. He would come to my store "to report." I would have arranged for food and lodging for him. He never demanded a nickel and never spent one either. And he always insisted on staying at the cheapest boarding houses. When he wasn't tracking down a donation, he could be seen on the busiest main street corners standing on a wooden Coca Cola box (which I kept in the store) so people could hear him better and see him more easily. He always had a crowd listening as he repeated his plea for help, Bible opened in his hand.

One of our Salvation Army programs was a monthly used-clothing drive. A Salvation Army truck came up from Minneapolis for a citywide pickup. To make it easier for some givers, I set up a dumpster behind my store where people could drop off clothing. The truck drivers were generally recovering alcoholics the Salvation Army had helped.

Once a used-clothing collection truck I had called for came up with "saved" and "recovered alcoholic" truck drivers who had promised to refrain from drinking. The collection was scheduled and widely publicized for a Monday. So these two drivers requested the Minneapolis Salvation Army headquarters to allow them to come to Little Falls Saturday and Sunday to camp out before the all-day collection Monday.

They came up Saturday and reported to me at 9:00 a.m. at my store. I told them to go to Sweeney's gas station and fill up with gas and have Sweeney call me and I would bring him a check for the gas.

At 2:00 p.m. I got a frantic telephone call from Sweeney. Lacing his speech with expletives, he asked, "Joe, you still head of the Salvation Army?"

I said, "Yes."

He said, "Well, maybe you'll want to quit right now. You'd better send me a helluva big check because after I filled the 30-gallon tank with gas, they plowed into one of my gas pumps. They bruised it up so it'll never work again. And they hit it twice!"

My store was loaded with customers as I pushed out the back door, jumped in my car and rushed to the station. The drivers had done a great job of destruction. They were completely bombed. With bottles in hand, they lay in the back of the truck, singing with raspy voices that penetrated the quiet of the neighborhood.

I finally quieted them down and drove the truck to the park where they had pitched their tents and where they had already ruined the midday serenity of the tourists who were trying to enjoy the quiet wilderness. I read the riot act to them and told them that they had one day to sober up and report to me at the store Monday morning at 8:00 a.m. sharp.

Few of my friends and relatives have knowledge of my

involvement and experiences with the charitable work of the Salvation Army. I received no compensation or personal gain. I did receive a national award from the Salvation Army for outstanding work in the United States. I also received a letter from Hubert Humphrey, while he was Vice President.

My greatest reward was the satisfaction I experienced helping the poor. This work electrifies mind and body when you give of yourself and your assets to help unfortunates. My wife, Olive, describes it as an "inner glow" when we get prepared to do our works of charity.

Uncle Joe

I have spent my whole life loving children — mine, those of my relatives, and my wonderful friends' children. I've hugged, kissed, and encouraged them throughout my life.

From 1968 to 1975 I spearheaded and chaired a yearly financial drive to augment the meager budget of St. Mary's Grade School in Little Falls, Minnesota. This drive was a one-day bike ride for which the kids solicited donors who would pay them so much a mile. At the conclusion of the event, we had a huge gathering at the gym of parents and students for free food and drink and a circus-like celebration.

Before the big event, I used to leave the Penney store at least twice a week to go to the school gym at St. Mary's where the children sat on the floor waiting for Uncle Joe to come to give them a "pep talk." I'd roll up my right trouser leg to the knee (like a biker), walk in and get 250 kids to yell, "We're Number One!" I'd give them words of encouragement and a sales pitch. The first year we raised over $10,000 in one day.

In 1982, I lost my beloved wife, Dorothy, and became a permanent resident of Phoenix, Arizona. I remarried to one of her great friends, Olive (Annie) Gill from Canada and in 1986, Annie and I visited Little Falls. Sister Willenbring, who was the principal at St. Mary's when I was actively involved, was still there ten years later. When she learned that we were coming to Little Falls she asked if I would please come up to the gym and give the kids another pep talk.

My wife and I went to the school. With Sister Joyce, we stood near the doors to the gym. The nuns and lay teachers led their students in and, as they were about to enter, the kids saw me. I hadn't been there for four years, but they broke out of their organized lines and started screaming, "There's Uncle Joe! There's Uncle Joe! There's Uncle Joe!" And they began hugging my legs, still yelling. My wife's eyes popped open in disbelief. I swallowed hard, took a deep breath and entered the gym to face the bedlam. They are truly Number One!

St. Vincent de Paul

My wife and I belong to a group of volunteers for St. Vincent de Paul in downtown Phoenix. As one of its many charities, S.V.D.P. serves an average of one thousand full hot meals every day to the poor, crippled, and destitute in our main dining room. Our turn is Friday and we work in the kitchen filling the plates with a full-course dinner. This is not a soup kitchen! It's interesting that, as I lead a short prayer while the hungry sit down, in eight years I have rarely seen a person make the sign of the cross, bow a head, or join hands in prayer — most just keep on eating.

We have never proselytized. In 1991 in Phoenix, 65 Catholic church parishioners donated over one million dollars to clothe and feed the poor, most of whom have no religion. Of that, only $35,000 was spent for administrative purposes. Just think!

Ninety-seven percent of what we collected went directly to the poor. Show me any charitable organization in the world with that kind of record. If our government assumed this task it would probably take in nothing, spend $50,000,000, and hire 1,200 employees to do the job. In 1991, in Phoenix alone, our volunteers made 25,000 home visits and gave 300,000 hours in service.

Many of our volunteers have good jobs and take time during their "off hours" or "off days" to help. And many are retirees who feel a strong urge and obligation to help these unfortunates. As our chief executive officer, Christ, said, "What you do to the least of my brethren you do to me."

Our volunteers, with no financial reward, are a tremendous source of help for dining rooms, satellite feeding stations, food banks, reclamation centers, free medical and dental clinics, free barbering, family counseling, and our thrift stores. We have dozens of trucks that go out every day to pick up donated day-old bread, assorted pastries, canned goods, meats, and fruit at grocery chains and independents who support our cause. Every year we provide more than 1,000,000 full hot meals (6,000 a day) in our main dining room and satellite feeding stations in and around the Phoenix area.

We have our big annual food drive before Thanksgiving every year. In 1991, 41,000 empty grocery bags were handed out to Catholic parishioners at all masses in eighty-five Catholic churches in Phoenix during one weekend. They returned 28,912 bags the next weekend with food for the poor and needy, and $97,961 in cash. Each bag averaged $12.50 in value. The total value came to $459,361 — in one weekend!

S.V.D.P. operates in fifty-seven countries. In the United States it operates in 174 Catholic dioceses, but only a quarter of all parishes have a unit. The total U.S. membership is only 57,702, and another only 30,000 contribute. But in 1991, nationwide:

Total of persons helped - 7,854,236
Total served in their homes - 4,770,806
Total visited in institutions - 1,183,631
Total person to person aid - 1,899,804
Total hours of service by Vincentians - 12,283

S.V.D.P. began in Phoenix in 1962 when seven men rented a small, closed lunch counter with six stools. These volunteers took time from their work to go up and down the business district begging for food and rent money. They also begged from farmers nearby. They fed sixteen people the first day, ran out of food, begged the next day, fed and ran out of food, begged again. Every day the operation grew, attracting more poor and more volunteers. And just think! Today we serve good, hot, full meals. Every day. Just because we care.

I'm a charitable person, I think. I've tried my whole life to do something good for someone else (besides my family) — every day. I've also tried to promote that quality or virtue in others, especially young people. (I have this sensible idea that before I leave this earth I should replace myself). The young today say, "We don't have time or the money to do any charity now. We'll do it when we're like you — older."

What's older? To me older is seconds after you're born! I started serious charity when I was seventeen. What's your excuse?

St. Joseph's

My first effort to raise money for the church was one of the hardest. It taught me a lot about organizing and managing a successful fundraising campaign. A letter I wrote to solicit funds from the parish ...

Dear Fellow Catholics:

Our church is falling apart. The back of the church is bulging out with loose bricks and mortar, the window casings are so loose in their frames that the wind is blowing through, the steps are crumbling, and the sacristy is in ill repair. If this were our own home, we would repair it ourselves or pay someone else to do it. Well, this is our spiritual home, where we are born in baptism and borne in death. It is our home — every brick — every chunk of mortar — every nail — every piece of timber. We own it!

Since it belongs to us and we cannot fix it ourselves, we must pay to have it repaired. This letter goes begging for the most important financial drive in our lives in 1953 — the building fund for our church.

We need almost $3,000 for immediate repairs, and we want to raise enough to have a reserve to draw on for future repairs.

This letter is intended only to raise money for the repair of our church. And when it is collected no amount more than $300 can be spent without the unanimous consent of the Board of Trustees, composed of the Bishop, the Vicar General, Father Cashen, S.E. Koop, and Mike Gillespie, the latter two representing the parish to ensure the money is spent wisely and in accordance with our wishes.

Now, there are many ways to raise funds. We can flood the town with bingo parties, raffles, church suppers, waste paper collections, rummage sales, bake sales, card parties, and so forth. These are all worthwhile church functions and we will want to continue some of them to augment the treasuries of our various church organizations. However, we would have to sponsor twenty-five to thirty-five separate events this year to raise enough to make the immediate, necessary repairs. And you can imagine the work that would create: heading committees, serving on committees, baking, betting, donating, selling and buying tickets — and still having to attend all the events. If that didn't work, we would end up going door-to-door, which is embarrassing to both giver and receiver.

To eliminate all of this, we are offering a simple plan that we know you will approve. Please note the pledge card that is attached. We would like you to pledge for the year 1953 a certain amount to the building fund alone. It must be a separate amount, in addition to what you normally give in any one year. The church still needs your Sunday collections for the normal running expenses during the year.

How much should you pledge? No one can tell you. You contribute from your heart, your conscience, and your ability to pay. This letter is not a bill and must not be construed as such. We think some of our American heritage is destroyed when parishioners cannot contribute what they desire of their own free will.

However, if every wage earner in our parish would contribute an amount less than the cost of a daily cup of coffee, seven cents a day, about $25.00 a year, we will have attained our building fund goal. We hope that some may wish to contribute more — maybe two, three, or four cups of coffee a day.

How will you pay? At the bottom of your enclosed pledge card, you will find four suggestions. You may choose the one that satisfies you.

All contributions are tax-deductible and all pledges and payments will be listed separately from the Sunday collections on the financial statement that Father proposes to send to every wage earner in the parish.

In conclusion, we of the building committee would like to say that this is not Father Cashen's idea, nor does he know of our program. We didn't know him before his coming to Crosby, so there has been no affiliation of any sort. We alone have undertaken this program to relieve him of the unpleasantness of begging from the altar Sunday after Sunday, or of trying to solicit funds himself. We have been blessed with a sincere, hardworking, intelligent, and humble parish priest whose every prayer and daily task are for one purpose — to help us live and keep our faith.

All information in this letter has been explained to the Lady Forresters, the Altar Society and the Knights of Columbus. It has met with unanimous approval and consent of all three organizations.

We should like to surprise Father Cashen by presenting all cash, checks, and pledges to him at a one-hour coffee social in the church basement Thursday, March 19 — the birthday of St. Joseph, the patron Saint of our church. Every adult in the parish should try to attend that night.

Time is short and there is so much to do after your pledges arrive that we beg you to return the pledges promptly. A self-addressed, stamped envelope is enclosed for your convenience.

On behalf of our parish, we would like to thank you most sincerely for taking time to read this letter and we would like to express our heartfelt appreciation for any pledges you make. Remember: be generous, this is your church!

J. J. DeBevec
Chairman, 1953 Building Committee

Blessings

My involvement with St. Mary's grade school in Little Falls, Minnesota returned to me many blessings, none greater than the outpouring of sympathy and affection showered on me when my wife Dorothy died in 1982. I received 250 individual letters and cards of condolence from St. Mary's school children. From kindergarten through the eighth grade — in all shapes of paper and colors, printed, written, scrawled, in ink, pencil, and crayon. Some drew pictures of their childhood visions of heaven, Jesus, and God. Many of the children came to the funeral, which was a beautiful show of support for our family. Here are a few of these precious gems exactly as they were written:

Dear Uncle Joe, I'm so sorry your wife died. That was so fun those other years you came and gave us a pep talk. You'd always shake our hands and throw the little kids on your back. It was so fun to have you come and visit us sometime. Love, Amy, Grade 4

Dear Uncle Joe, I am very sorry for you. I am sorry it had to happen. But it will happen to everyone. We're working on raising marathon money. So far I raised $12. We miss you on the marathon. Love, Luann

Dear Uncle Joe, I am sorry it had to happen. You have my sympathy. Thank you for all that you did for our school and for me. I will always remember you. Love, Sarah

Dear Uncle Joe, I'm new in the class. I am from Wis. Even thoe I love you, Paul

Dear Uncle Joe, We are sorry to hear that your wife died. You will miss her very much. We will say some special prayers for her, and for you, and your family. God give you the strength and courage to be brave and strong. Your friends in the 2nd Grade, St. Mary's School

Dear Uncle Joe, I am sorry that your wife died and hope you cheer up really, really, fast! From, Kelly

Remarkable People

"The fruit of faith is love, and the fruit
of love is service to others."
— Mother Teresa

Juan Joe Fernandez

ONE OF THE PEOPLE I HAVE MET working for S.V.D.P. has made a strong impression on me. I want you to meet Juan Joe Fernandez, a paid worker in the kitchen of St. Vincent De Paul where we serve the poor. I have rarely seen such exuberance, vitality, alacrity, and willingness to do any job. He can do the work of two big men by himself, with a continual smile.

Let me tell you his story as he told it to me. He was born in Mexico of poor parents. His mother died giving birth to him. His father, a soldier, raised Juan alone, until he was six years old, when his father died. As their only child, he was left with no relations, poorly clothed, and with no education. So he struck out on his own — at age six! He lived on garbage, rotten food from grocery stores, he begged and borrowed, did odd jobs every day, and at night slept anywhere. Homeless, he lived in this impoverished state for nine years.

At the age of fifteen, he joined the army as his father had. This gave him an enviable life of free food, clean uniforms and a bed. But at eighteen, he quit and went out on his own, repeating his pre-army life. Finally, he managed to get to the U.S. border from Mexico City, a long, long way. He walked and ran as there weren't many cars in those days to pick him up and the shortest way to cover the 500 miles was a straight line through the desert.

When he finally reached the border and he saw the huge Rio Grand River — Madre Mia! He couldn't swim! But he found some Mexican men he could hire for a few pesetas to carry him on their shoulders until it got deep and then drag him across by swimming. He then had to evade the customs and get to some American city, so he sweet-talked a driver into taking him.

He came to Phoenix at nineteen years old without money, food, housing, or clothes except those he was wearing. For sixteen years, he scrounged a living as an illegal alien. He stood in the S.V.D.P. food line many times until he asked for a job. Then, at age thirty-four, as a kitchen worker, he was paid nothing, but he got a full breakfast and all the food he could eat for dinner. He cleaned up and left at 3:00 p.m., and had no more to eat that day.

His daily regimen was to wander the city, looking at shop windows, going to the library to read the Spanish newspapers, and brushing up on his English. Then at darkness, he would start looking for a place to sleep. He had no pack or bag, and only the one set of clothes he was wearing. He slept on open ground, park benches, and culverts. But his favorite spot was an abandoned building where he could curl up alone to fend off the chill. He had a wrist watch someone gave him. At 6:00 a.m., he would get up in the clothes he slept in, walk to the S.V.D.P. dining room, where he could take a shower and begin another day.

He was such a good worker that finally S.V.D.P. hired him as a paid employee. Now that we're good friends, he has taken me into his confidence. One day he told me he had received his first paycheck since his army days seventeen years ago. I asked him how much he made. He said he didn't know. He took his unopened pay envelope out of his pocket and asked me to open it and tell him. I told him it was $403 for a month's work. He said "Holy smokes. I'm rich!"

Ida Mae Holland

This black woman was born in 1944 in Greenwood, Mississippi, the daughter of a local midwife who eked out a sparse living helping those who couldn't afford doctors. Ida Mae never knew her father, although many of her mother's boyfriends called themselves dad. At age thirteen, she became a prostitute and worked her trade until she was eighteen years old in 1962, when she followed a prospect to Freedom House (a nonviolent committee working for racial justice).

For three years she worked all over the U.S. for the civil rights movement, getting paid $14 a week. In 1965, she came home to visit her mother in Greenwood and as she approached, saw her mother's home burn to the ground, her mother dying in flames on the doorstep. Ida Mae stayed there for three years to complete high school at the age of twenty-one and then headed for the University of Minnesota in Minneapolis. She founded a prison aid program and because she worked at this for little pay, she didn't get to finish college until twelve years later, in 1979.

She was thirty-five years old. She then wrote a play called "Second Doctor Lady from the Mississippi Delta." It played on Broadway and was extremely successful. Afterwards, she started to work on her doctorate and received her Ph.D. in 1985. It took her six years. She is now a professor of Womens Studies at the University of Buffalo in New York.

I, as a colored person (white) take my hat off to a colored person (black) and hope that all colors reading this will realize that if she made it, anyone can. You just have to be willing to suffer enough, as she did.

Mother Teresa

Agnes Bojaxhiu was born in Skopje, Yugoslavia, the daughter of a very prosperous merchant. At the age of eighteen, a mere five-foot slip of a girl, she entered the Irish Order of Loretto, taking the name of Teresa as a tribute to the "Little Flower" of Lisieux, to whom she was fervently devoted. On January 6, 1929, she arrived in Calcutta, India. For sixteen years she wore the black veil of the nuns of her congregation, teaching geography to the daughters of well-to-do Bengali families.

In 1946, on a train ride, "the voice of God resounded in my ears and gave me an order. I was to leave the comfort of my convent and give up everything to follow Jesus Christ into the slums and to serve Him in the distressing disguise of the poorest of the poor."

Her mother superior, the archbishop of Calcutta, and the whole hierarchy joined forces to make her give up the project. They argued that this "call" was probably no more than a hallucination brought on by fatigue. But she was unwavering. She wrote to Rome and after two years, finally received the Holy Father's permission. And in 1948, with Jacqueline de Decker and a companion, she started the "Missionary of Charity" Order.

And, of course, you know what happened then. She and her sisters have ministered to millions of poor and dying and she has received the Nobel Peace Prize.

I sometimes wonder, if she hadn't taken that train ride, what would have happened?

Here is another story about her:

Mother Teresa announced that she wanted to open an establishment for dying AIDS patients in New York. She came to New York to found a house for such a purpose and was directed to meet with the mayor, Ed Koch, with whom she had a long conversation.

He told her he already had a huge building suitable for her hospice in downtown New York. Mother said, "Downtown New York? I want a house in the country, not downtown. All over India, scattered homes for the dying are operated by thousands of lepers who work the soil, farm fish, raise chickens, and raise crops."

Koch said, "Dear Mother, these dying AIDS patients can't even stand. They are not qualified as farmers, carpenters, or plumbers."

Mother Teresa said, "If lepers who have lost their fingers, hands, feet, faces, noses, and ears can manage to build their own homes and work their crops, why shouldn't Americans with all four limbs do the same?"

Mayor Koch said he had never in his life seen such a persistent person. Before she left, Mother Teresa pressed a small piece of paper in his hand on which she had scribbled these words: "The fruit of silence is prayer. The fruit of prayer is faith. The fruit of faith is love, and the fruit of love is service to others."

Jacqueline de Decker

Here is a digest of a terrific book, Beyond Love by Dominique LaPierre, the author of City of Joy:

Jacqueline de Decker, at eighteen, was a beautiful rich young woman, daughter of prominent citizens of Antwerp, Belgium. As an attractive marriage prospect, her beauty and position turned many a head. However, she preferred to shut herself in a chapel for hours each day in the belief that God wanted her to enter a religious order. In 1939, she packed her suitcase and left for the convent of the Missionary Sisters of Mary in Calcutta, determined to dedicate herself to God in India to care for the poorest of the poor, but as a lay worker.

A Belgian priest had opened a medical center in an impoverished area in Madras, and she went there to join it. She was told that she needed further schooling, so she returned to Antwerp, just as Hitler was shattering Belgium. She joined the Red Cross, earned her nursing diploma, and served through four years in over-worked hospitals.

In August 1946, now qualified, she returned to the hospital in Madras. The Belgian priest had died so she took over, but was all alone. She lived and worked among the poorest of the poor in an impoverished dispensary. Her daily meal was a bowl of rice seasoned with chili beans and some cups of tea. She slept on bare earth in a wooden hovel infested with rats and cockroaches. She administered to tuberculosis sufferers, lepers, and countless poor.

One day she heard about a European nun who had left her convent in Calcutta to form a new religious order that would take care of sick, crippled, or dying street children and beggars, and give shelter to all the abandoned. Jacqueline de Decker met Sister Teresa on August 8, 1948. The nun asked Jacqueline to join her as her first assistant in establishing what is now the world-famous Missionaries of Charity order, which now has branches in nearly every country in the world.

Shortly after the formation, Jacqueline was suddenly crippled with spinal pain, a result of a diving accident at the age of fifteen. Her condition worsened and she had to return to Belgium, where she suffered months in hospitals. She had fifteen operations to try to save her from complete paralysis. In the end, she was imprisoned from the nape of her neck to the base of her hips in a plastic corset. She wrote Mother Teresa a heart-rending letter telling her that the meaning of life was slipping away from her.

Shortly after, she received an aerogram from Mother Teresa, who asked Jacqueline to be the mother of a unique project. This would create a mystical link of communion between physical sufferers who need to be active and those active persons who need their prayers. Jacqueline's body would be in Belgium and her soul in India. Jacqueline immediately formed the link for sick and suffering co-workers of Mother Teresa, affiliated to the Missionaries of Charity, a chain of love that would encircle the world like a rosary. She convinced twenty-seven severely disabled or incurably ill people in Belgium to become twin sisters to the first twenty-seven sisters who formed Mother Teresa's Missionaries of Charity.

Today, forty years later, Jacqueline de Decker, still in her straitjacket of pain, coordinates the Worldwide Communion of Souls from her apartment in Antwerp. Thousands of sick people join in prayer and the offering of their suffering to Missionaries of Charity who are working for the dying all over the world.

Retirement

You have to keep going because if you accept
the end, you lose.
— Quarterback Ken Stabler

Senior Olympics

IN JULY OF 1985, when I was seventy years old, I entered
the World Masters' Senior Olympics, to be held in Toronto the following month. Of the twenty-six sports, I chose swimming (breast
stroke) and entered only one event — the grueling one-mile.

I had never trained for or competed in a swimming contest
in my life. I didn't know what to expect so I swam hard and long
every day at our condo pool in Toronto to prepare for the event.

The meet was held at the Canadian National Olympic
swimming arena at Etobicoke, a suburb of Toronto. Twenty-five
hundred swimmers from sixty-two countries came to compete.
Most of them were former world and Olympic contestants and
champions. They entered the arena in teams, with warmup suits
and embroidered swim trunks, luxurious satin jackets and pants,
and the finest in footwear, followed by a swarm of personal doctors, rubdown specialists, trainers, timers, equipment managers,
and supporters. I gazed, open-mouthed, at all this splendor. I sat
alone on a bare bench at the end of the 50-meter pool clothed only
in an old, faded, baggy swim trunk. I asked myself: "What am I
doing here? I've got to cut this short, or I'll start to cry."

I entered in lane 1, heat 7 and finished the mile in fifty-one minutes, ten seconds, placing sixth in the world for a bronze medal.

With newfound confidence, I looked for more opportunities to compete as a master swimmer. I read in the Phoenix, Arizona daily newspaper the next January of an Arizona State Senior Olympics for ages fifty-five to eighty-five. I could enter a total of three events. I chose the 100-yard, 500-yard, and the one-mile events. They would award three medals in each race — bronze for third, silver for second, and gold for first.

I surprised myself by winning a silver in the 100-yard. I had barely composed myself when I got the call to enter the 500-yard. I huffed and puffed my way through, and won a bronze.

The monster — the 1,760-yard mile — was last. While I was warming up, I developed severe leg cramps. Not in the water — on the bench! I hobbled to one of the coaches who hurriedly lowered me to the pavement and started working on my legs. He relieved the pain, so I got up and said five Our Fathers and five Hail Marys and got into the pool. The gun barked and I took off.

In the lane next to me was Joe Linsallata from New Jersey. He was my age and the gold medal winner the past two years. We had to swim sixty-six lengths of the 25-meter pool. After my 4th length, water flooded my right goggle lens and I couldn't see out of it at all. Sixty-two more lengths to go! Fearful that every stroke and every quick turn would flood the other lens and blind me completely and disqualify me, I swam very cautiously. Now, to compete cautiously in a sport that requires speed is absolutely ridiculous. But I am not a quitter. I beat Linsallata by seven lengths and won the gold medal. (Cautiously of course).

Canadian

(A tale of extreme patience — little of which I possess.)

In 1984, after marriage to my present lovely bride in Canada, I was informed by immigration authorities that to qualify as a landed immigrant in Canada, without relinquishing my US citizenship, I would have to establish a permanent residency there in Toronto. I would then qualify for all the amenities of a Canadian citizen except pensions, since I hadn't contributed anything toward it. But I learned that a ten-year backlog of applicants from all over the world meant I would have a long wait. The immigration service suggested I apply through the Canadian embassy and immigration office in Los Angeles, where applicants were few. Then I could get it through in two years, when I would be seventy-two. I wrote the Canadian embassy in Los Angeles a pleasant letter. They wrote me a pleasant letter informing me that I would have to make a personal appearance — not once but often.

I wrote them another pleasant letter. I explained to them the difficulty of my making a personal appearance many times because of the distance involved. The head of the Canadian embassy personally wrote me a pleasant letter telling me I was going to be awarded a special dispensation and could apply from Phoenix, where I lived. However, I would be required to file many forms by mail. Eventually, they required that I send them twenty-seven different forms that included:

1. My lifetime involvement in all endeavor since grade school;
2. Statements from police departments that I had never been arrested in the last three cities in which I lived;
3. Copies of both marriage certificates;
4. Copies of death certificates of both of our former spouses;
5. Financial reports from all financial institutions, banks, stock funds, mutual funds, or other investments;

6. Copy of my driver's license;

7. Copies of both my wife's passport and my own;

8. Proof of medical, life, and accident insurance policies;

9. Witness statements — American and Canadian;

10. Discharge papers from the U.S. Army;

11. Complete physical examination reports from American and Canadian doctors.

But I persevered and broke all Canadian records by finishing them in one year.

Hockey Again

My wife's first husband, Ernie Gill, retired as inspector of detectives in the police force of Toronto and died an early death at sixty-two. Since I married his Canadian wife, I now spend a third to a half of my life in Canada and I've heard a lot about him. But, I have never — I repeat — never been irritated by any of the many discussions I've heard about him. In fact, I have encouraged them. I admired him and his profession and have always spoken highly of him.

Ernie was one big man. I am 6'3" and weigh 185 pounds with a 35-inch waist. He was 6'1" weighing 220 pounds with a 44-inch waist. After I married Olive, I found that all of his clothes were still in the closet. I hadn't brought any clothes to Canada from the U.S. to "grub in," so I put on his pants, boots, stockings, jacket, and gloves to work around the house, which is unoccupied much of the time. I had no hesitation about wearing them. Of course, I looked like a scarecrow, as I pinned the excess inches of his pants, and his jackets and coats were enormous on me. I looked like I was sent for and didn't come.

One day in 1985 I went to see the Queen of England and her husband who were visiting Toronto. They came in their huge ship "Britannia" and docked at the harbor. I had brought no jacket from the U.S., so I put on one of Ernie's warm sweaters, a baseball-type cap with a large emblem, "Toronto Metro Police," on the front. Then I put on one of Ernie's yellow nylon sport jackets, which had the name of a junior hockey team emblazoned on the back and a very conspicuous "Ernie Gill" with crossed hockey sticks on the front. He had volunteered as a police-sponsored hockey coach during off-duty hours.

So, onto the subway I went to meet the Queen. Of course, everyone in Toronto had the same idea. They jammed us behind a huge chain fence with heavily guarded gates, which separated us from the dock area. Because of tight security, the area was filled with police officers, patrol cars, ambulances, and motorcycle police. I passed many officers on my way to get near to the gang plank. They all noticed my police cap and I received salutes, smiles, and warm greetings from my "fellow officers." I was trying to get as close as possible for the best camera shots. I was a long way from succeeding until a police officer guarding inside the fence noted my cap, and yelled "Sir, this way," and politely urged people to step aside. He guided me to a fence opening for an uncluttered view of the Queen — an excellent camera shot.

During the wait, a man next to me noticed my jacket back and front and, with a warmth unusual for a Canadian, said "I'm Jack Ferguson" and I said "Hi, I'm Ernie Gill." He was also a coach in a similar hockey league and he wanted to compare notes. Well, no one could have been better prepared than I, and I proved my expertise. Eveleth was the birthplace of hockey in the U.S. and is today the home of the USA hockey Hall of Fame. There was little I didn't know about the game and so Jack and "Ernie" sailed into a long discussion of hockey — its rules, strategy, coaching, offense, defense, famous Canadian and American hockey heroes — everything! Ernie would have been proud of me!

Chain Saw

Every summer we have a long stay at our daughter Carol's and her husband Al's summer home on Lake Ontario. One year, I spent a few days collecting driftwood logs and piles of fallen limbs that had come down in a windstorm. I like to keep the fireplace going in September and October and didn't want to use their precious firewood; I wanted to burn my own.

On the third day, I got up early to chain saw — no swimming, no sunning, no reading, no goofing off. Before leaving for the summer, Al had shown me his new electric chain saw. He told me, "You don't have to worry about this one." (The previous saw burned out in my hands. I was just looking at it). He said, "If the chain gets loose it won't cut, so just loosen the two nuts on the sprocket, pull the chain tight, tighten the nuts again, and it will work for some time." Simple!

Anything mechanical hates me. As soon as I touch it, it malfunctions. After fighting those miserable contraptions for more than twenty years, I viewed this one with doubt and apprehension. But I arranged the wood on sawhorses, pressed the trigger, and cut an inch into the log. The chain stuck. I finally extricated it and the blade was on but hanging like a cooked piece of spaghetti.

So I loosened the nuts, tightened the blade, and lunged at the cut in the log. This time, I only cut half way through and it stuck again. I see the limp blade hanging down in a curve.

Canadian saws are different from American saws, to which I was accustomed. So I felt a need for some expert advice. Burt Branscombe lives about three blocks away and is an absolute expert on anything mechanical. So I walked to his place with the chain saw.

Now, Burt is an absolute prince and I love him, but unfortunately, he had a stroke a few years ago. His mind is brilliant as ever and his eyes are sharp and clear. But the stroke has left him with a slow shuffle, impaired speech, and unsteady hands. And he is deaf. His movement and speech are very slow and he chews a big wad of tobacco. So I was resigned to spending a long time.

The first thing Burt said as we approached his garage was, "We've got to have a beer." When he finally came back from the house with the beer, he said, "Well, we have to sit and sip to think this over." Since his hands trembled so much, he put a straw into the bottle and clamped it with a clothespin so it wouldn't slip down. As the beer got lower, he adjusted the straw by lowering it and raising the clothespin. He sipped for what seemed like hours.

Burt's tool shop in his garage would be the envy of General Motors. He has every tool imaginable, from a three-foot pipe wrench to a probing tool as small as a needle. But they are not in order— his tables are covered with them. So we had a comedy of errors.

Burt is deaf with one hearing aid. I am deaf with two hearing aids. I was talking too fast. Burt was talking reeeeal slow, and his shifting tobacco wad was not helping. Our exchange of assistance was hilarious. We took the chain saw all apart. The chain kept slipping off, so we unscrewed the hood and got it back on. Then we spilled our beers among the tools.

Back to the house for another two beers. Then we worked on the innards of the saw, trying to adjust a screw little bigger than a pinhead in a sea of sawdust.

Then came the flies. There is no insect in the world as vicious, obnoxious, or with a worse bite than a common Canadian fly in September and October. They bit us on the arms, legs, face, and especially our hands as we tried various screw drivers in the bowels of the chain saw. We used fly swatters — missed every one. Then we sprayed "Off" — no luck. We sprayed insect repellent — they flew through that mist like dive bombers, sucked in every droplet, and loved it. It made them declare full war.

We finally got the chain saw adjusted, put back the housing, and got a piece of wood in a vice to test it. Rrrrr! It didn't even scratch the bark.

Burt said, "We'll try my chain saw." We did. His didn't scratch the bark either. So we thought maybe both chains were dull. After ten minutes, Burt found the chain saw sharpener. Into the vise with the chains. I sharpened them both. We tested them on wood — again, barely a bruise on the bark.

I had gone there at 9:00 a.m. and now it was 3:15 p.m. We decided that maybe we should have a newer chain. I ran back three blocks, took apart Al's last year's model that had burned out, removed the chain, and ran back three blocks with it. We took it apart, put it together, tested it. Zilch!

More flies, more mumbling, more beer, more frustration. Finally Burt got out his strong magnifying glass, which he uses for fine detail work, and discovered that we had been putting in all the chains backwards! The cutting points weren't running forward so the chains weren't cutting anything.

Just think! The sharpest engine technician anywhere, and me with twenty years of chain saw experience doing something as stupid as that. So we took Al's saw apart and put it together again. We tested it on a 4-inch diameter log in a vise; it ripped through it in a fifth of a second. By then, we had been on this for eight hours, a job that should have taken ten minutes. But as Burt said, "You've got to be patient!"

Happy Hour

I have never been in love with a bar, although I'm sure they fulfill some useful purposes. There are millions of them for the mass of people who spew out of work at 5 o'clock and make a mad dash for their favorite happy hour. As a father and a husband, I believed my family deserved something better, so I had my happy hour at home. When it was time for dinner, I was never late. When Mother said "Dinner!", I didn't have to move. I was already there.

My wife Annie and I still look forward to our before-dinner cocktail hour every day at 4:30 (don't call us — we'll call you). It's our magic hour to put our feet up on the cocktail table (imitation wood from Woolco, on sale for $69.95). We thoroughly enjoy the relaxing time, without the raucous cacophony of bar noise.

She will have two drinks and I the same. It's our magic hour to discuss everything that is meaningful to us. The TV is never on then. So we talk, about anything and everything. If we had to be separated during the day, our serious conversations are augmented by discussions on hot buys we got at the grocery store, the sale bargains at Penney's, the specials on liquor at Walgreen's, what we found in the dumpsters, how well the prune juice is working, a friend finding a condom in our outdoor Jacuzzi. . . . You know — really important subjects.

It's our own private bar so:

We never get drunk.

We never hurt anyone.

We never fight anyone.

We never maim anyone.

We never kill anyone.

We never argue.

And we never get carried away with the bar girl or the bar boy.

And finally, there's an old Irish saying: "I'm never drunk until I can't recognize my wife." Well, gentle reader, I can surely recognize my wife. She's the cute thing sitting across from me at dinner. And I'm never late!

A Contrast in Living

In Canada we enjoy a quiet, heavily-wooded peninsula jutting out into the east end of Lake Ontario. In all directions, we see a vast expanse of whitecaps on clear blue water.

And then, three hours later, we can sit on the balcony of our modern condo in metropolitan Toronto overlooking the city and find ourselves gazing at a panorama of high-rise apartments and office buildings, listening to the steady roar of traffic, blaring horns, and screaming sirens. What a contrast! What a life!

A Beautiful Sight

We had some beautiful neighbors in Phoenix who lived below us on the ground floor of our apartment complex near Thomas and 36th Street. Their drapes were open all the time, so their lives were an open book to many who passed by. I often went down and they would have me in. We'd have a discourse on how to settle all the world's ills. They are outstanding people with strong Christian beliefs. At the time, Tim was ninety and Lena was eighty, both healthy, energetic, interesting, lovable. One day, I passed by their window and the lights were on. I could see Tim sitting on one end of their long couch, his wife stretched out full-length with her head in his lap, her eyes closed. Tim was watching TV and stroking and stroking his wife's beautiful, pure white hair. I couldn't go in — why louse up such a beautiful sight?

Faith

The assurance of things hoped for and
the conviction of things not seen.

Candles

PEOPLE WHO DON'T UNDERSTAND the Catholic faith find it
difficult to understand what they consider the folderol of our lighting candles in the sanctuary of the church or our home. They probably believe it's a moneymaking operation or a heathen practice.
Not true — for thousands of years in caves, churches, temples and
other places of worship, your predecessors lit candles to glorify a
deity and to remember a sacred event or those who passed on.
Non-Catholics light candles at the table for important dinner gath-
erings, because it creates an ambiance. It has no other significance
to you. But when we put a buck in the slot to pay for the candle
and light it in a church, it's to remind us of the Lord saying "Let
there be light" and usually to remember someone we loved who
passed away. When we strike the match and ignite the wick, we get
a lovely feeling for the good of the person for whom we lighted the
candle. We pause then, to pray for them.

My wife and I have traveled all over the world in more
countries that I care to count. We find a Catholic church and we
always light a candle for Dorothy DeBevec (my Catholic first
wife) and for Ernie Gill (my present wife's Protestant first hus-

band). And then we pray for them and then we smile as we reminisce about them. There's nothing wrong with our intent. He was a wonderful father and grandfather. And I include him without fail in my prayers every night and at Sunday mass, which I never miss.

Il Papa

In 1985, I was in Toronto for our usual six months there. My wife was away on a trip "with the girls" and the Pope was coming to town. For millions of Catholics, seeing the Pope is a once-in-a-lifetime experience. (For me it wasn't, though, as I first met the Pope in Rome in 1975 and was to meet him again in Phoenix in 1988.) His parade route was published, so I knew where the closest and most advantageous position would be. I got up early and filled my backpack with fruit and goodies, a book, and my rosary. I took the bus, the subway, and another bus to the corner I had chosen, where there was a small fast-food store with round concrete tables.

Two teenage girls were standing on a high table with a clear view for blocks in either direction. They were alone with their knapsacks, extra wraps, and packages of munchies. I hesitated to begin a greeting, in case they thought I was a dirty old man, but they yelled to come up, so I joined them on top of the table. What a sight! I was blessed with two good-looking surrogate grandchildren and they with an adopted grandfather.

We had a long wait so we decided to share our stories. They had exuberant personalities and a steady flow of sensible chatter. They asked me about my Canadian and American wives and children. I learned they were fifteen years old, attended a Catholic school four blocks away, worshiped their parents, had beautiful relationships with their siblings, worked after school and weekends, did charity work, and were absolutely thrilled to be able to see the Pope. They said it would be worth fifty times seeing Michael Jackson. They brought out pictures of parents, family, Catholic school, and school passes.

I had brought fruit and sandwiches and pop, but they had other plans. They were slim, but had the appetites of linebackers. They kept a steady pace of trips for popcorn, chips, cheese cups, munchies, and pop. My money was worthless. I was their guest and this was their treat.

Through all our discussions, we were aware of the gradual approach of thousands of people searching for a clear view of the Pontiff. People stood eight feet deep on every inch of sidewalk. Countless banners appeared to welcome the Pope in many foreign languages. The 6,000-member Toronto police force secured the entire parade route; I counted twelve police officers in our block alone. After three hours of anticipation, we could hear the roar of thousands of voices signaling his approach. The Pope suddenly breezed by in his Popemobile within ten feet of us. A quick camera click, and he was gone.

My new-found friendship with these delightful girls was not over. I promised to write them and I did. I received beautiful answers with notes by their parents. I have to think that on that beautiful sunny day, God brought his Vicar to us to let His light shine on a short-but-precious friendship between two exemplary young girls and a faithful veteran of life.

Abortion

According to the Arizona Republic, women in the U.S. are going to kill, by abortion, one and a half million babies in one year. That's one-half of one percent of our present population of 250 million. The same staggering statistic holds for Mexico. A quarter of a million babies will die by abortion in Canada in one year.

A hopeful irony: In May of 1991 in Phoenix, Arizona, a small child got lost in the desert. For three days, searchers scoured the desert — patrols, expert searchers, police, dogs, military planes, helicopters, the National Guard, and thousands of citizens. We spent millions of tax dollars to find one lost child in the Arizona desert. Yes, they found him — three days later — alive! And well! One child made it. However, this year alone millions of children will never get a chance to see the light of day.

In October 1982, when I was in Rochester, Minnesota undergoing medical tests, the TV and newspapers were giving full coverage to the whole nation for assistance in finding a heart for transplanting into a baby less than a year old. The father came on TV begging everyone in the U.S. for a suitable heart from a baby of the same age that died and whose parents were willing to donate the heart. Help and money poured in. Ads were donated for inserts in all media throughout the country. Private and government planes and helicopters were scouring the nation. Hundreds of doctors and nurses everywhere were involved and hospitals everywhere joined the search.

After what seemed an eternity, they finally found one in a western state; a baby had died and the parents offered the heart. A special transport plane was dispatched with dozens of highly trained technicians from Minneapolis. The little heart was flown back to the hospital. Dozens of hospital personnel greeted it. The total expense must have been a lot of money. The transplant was done. The next day the baby died. To pregnant mothers everywhere who are thinking about aborting — it was worth it!

Healing the Sick

Prayer is a very personal connection between yourself and God, a sincere invitation for God's life to be lived through you.

Prayer is the way to express your thanks for your life and its blessings, those you have received and those still to come. Prayer — anytime — is a time of worship, joy, and thanksgiving deep within your inner being. And after you've said it, your body and mind are renewed. You come away harmonized, revitalized, and at peace with yourself and with your world.

Scientific studies now prove what hospital chaplains, priests, ministers, and rabbis have long known, that prayer helps patients to get better and leave hospitals sooner. Other studies provide intriguing evidence that praying for other people can help even when the patients don't know that someone is putting in a good word for them. Studies also show that prayer after surgery leads to faster healing, not only for the "prayee," but also for the "prayor." I'm a veteran recovery patient and I truly believe that the constant prayers of my wife, my relatives, and my friends got me through. Of course, God and doctors work together to accomplish a successful result with medical expertise followed by comforting and healing with prayer.

Prayer

Our dear friend, Eileen Riordan, after a lifetime of nursing, firmly believes in prayer. She was a constant comfort to my wife, spending some time each day with her, and all day during the long operation to replace the aortic valve in my heart. Before the operation, compassionate Eileen comforted my wife by telling her, "Joey has so many people praying for him." I miraculously survived the operation that took a large team of dedicated nurses and doctors most of a day to complete and then survived complications that included three kidney failures. There was little chance that I would survive death, but good doctors and many prayers spared me again.

Family Tree

As I REVIEW MY LIFE, I've always had a funny feeling that I really don't know who I am, genealogically, that is. All I know is that I was born in the U.S. of poor parents who were born in Austria and spoke the Slovenian language. I never knew a grandparent. Where did my forefathers and foremothers come from?

I began reading history books on the migratory backgrounds of the Slavic people. As much as anywhere in the world, the Slavic republics experienced a continual mixing of nationalities and religions, mostly through wars as they met their enemies at their borders - clashed and fought, subjugated, intermarried, and gave birth to mixed ethnic children and then mixed ethnic nations - a melting pot of mixed nationalities.

Since the 1400s, this area has been mixed from inside and outside, conquered by the Turks, Austrians, Hungarians, French, Germans; with fighting between areas controlled by the the Serbs, Croats, Slavs, Czechs, Slovaks, and Slovenes.

In 1880 my dad was born and my mother in 1885 - about 100 kilometers from Ljubljana, the capital of Slovenia in what was

Austria-Hungary under the Hapsburg Dynasty under King Alexander. For me and my siblings, the ethnic mixing was finally over. Here are some interesting historical facts:

The Serbians lived in five southern Slav territories but not in Slovenia.

Many of the southern Slavs were of the Muslim faith because of long years of Turkish occupation, and many converted to Islam during the long years of occupation.

After World War I ended in 1918, the Serbs, Croats, and Slovenes formed a common kingdom and in 1929 renamed it Jugoslavia (Jugo means South and Slavia means all Southern Slavs). It then included 6 separate countries - Serbia, Croatia, Slovenia, Montenegro, Macedonia, Hercegovina, plus two provinces Vojuodina and Kosouo.

In 1994 the Slovenes and Croatians broke away and formed their own independent countries - Montenegro followed and then the war between the Serbs and the remaining countries ensued.

Serbs and Croats speak the same language and write it the same except the Serbs use Cyrillic lettering and the Croats use Latin.

The Slovenes speak a separate and different Slavic language but it is a cousin to the Serb and Croat one.

The Slovenes and Croats are Roman Catholic Christians and the Serbs are Byzantium Christians (Greek Orthodox).

Slovenian society is more industrialized than Serbs and Croats and has different class structure - one in which clericalism (Roman Catholic) and German language and culture carried great influence. In Slovenian regions, the German language was dominant beyond elementary school.

The Serbs for hundreds of years tried so arduously to keep the Slavic peoples a unified integral part of eastern Europe.

Family of Anton & Agnes DeBevec

For those DeBevec families all over the U.S. and still in Europe, I offer this genealogy of my family.

Father: Anton, Born in Austria on April 15, 1880. Died in Eveleth, Minnesota on September 7, 1965 at age eighty-five. Occupation: iron ore miner and later a janitor.

Mother: Agnes Petrich. Born in Austria on September 7, 1885. Died January 11, 1974 in Eveleth, Minnesota at age eighty-nine. Mother and Dad had one daughter, six sons, twenty-one grand-children, and thirty-one great grandchildren.

Sister: Agnes, born December 22, 1905. Died June 18, 1988 in Eveleth, Minnesota at age eighty-three. Occupation: homemaker. Husband: John Klemencic

Brother: Tony, born December 25, 1906 in Eveleth, Minnesota. Died September 6, 1994 at age eighty-seven. Occupation: iron ore pit assistant superintendent and explosives expert. Wife: Frances Debelak.

Brother: John, born March 14, 1908 in Eveleth, Minnesota. Died August 25, 1987 at age seventy-nine. Occupation: steam fitter, pipe fitter and welder. Wife: Bertha Bratulich.

Brother: Rudolph, born April 13, 1910 in Eveleth, Minnesota. Died May 10, 1992 at age eighty-two. Occupation: heavy equipment operator. Wife: Jennie Bratulich

Brother: Frank, born September 11, 1912 in Austria, Europe. Now eighty-two and still living. Occupation: electrician.

Brother: Joseph (the writer), born March 11, 1915. Occupation: J.C. Penney Co. assistant manager and manager for thirty-nine years. Wife: Dorothy Ann Mack (married 1940). Children: Jeffrey (b. 1947), Michael (b. 1951). Wife: Olive Gill (married 1984).

Brother: Louis, born May 16, 1917. Died February 20, 1988 at age seventy-one. Occupation: carpenter and cabinet maker.

What I did in my spare time since 1933:

1. High school class president.
2. President of Sigma Phi Alpha drama society in high school.
3. President of Delta Psi Omega drama society in college.
4. Member and officer of three academic organizations in college.
5. Employed as stock boy, sales associate, section manager, assistant manager and store manager for the J.C. Penney Co. stores for thirty-nine years in ten different stores and communities, in four states.
6. President of three Chambers of Commerce in different cities.
7. Member of St. Francis Convert research board.
8. Financial adviser to Catholic churches in ten communities.
9. School board member in two communities.
10. President of Salvation Army extension unit for twenty-five years.
11. Thirty years on financial boards for grade and high schools and colleges.
12. General financial chairman for the building of a University of Minnesota branch college in Morris, Minnesota.
13. Member and officer in Lions and Kiwanis service clubs in three cities.
14. Member of Elks Lodge for thirty years.

15. Member Officer Reserve Corps, U.S. Army.

16. Retired officer U.S. Army.

17. Served in U.S. Army for three years during World War II, including the European theater.

18. Member American Legion.

19. Member Veterans of Foreign Wars.

20. Member Disabled Veterans of U.S.

21. Member of St. Vincent de Paul for the Poor.

22. Lay minister at St. Theresa's in Phoenix, Arizona.

23. General Chair, financial drive for repairing church in Crosby, Minnesota.

24. General Chair of organ fund drive for church in Little Falls, Minnesota.

25. Board of Boy Scouts of America in three cities.

26. Area chair Elks camp for underprivileged children.

27. St. John's University associate for twenty years.

28. President Little Falls Country Club.

29. Lay Board member, St. John's Prep School.

30. One of the original five members of the planning committee to raise money for the new (1962) St. John's Prep school.

31. St. John's University financial committees.

32. United Fund board member for seven years.

33. Member Knights of Columbus for thirty years.

34. Installed the first bereavement program for widows and widowers at St. Theresa's Church in Phoenix, Arizona.

35. With my wife, served twelve years as Friday kitchen line managers of St. Vincent De Paul for The Poor to feed 1,000 poor a full hot meal every day.

The Gospel According to Joe

All successes and failures start at home.

Life

Nothing manufactured any more has a lasting quality. Remember refrigerators that lasted forty years, washing machines that never needed repairing? Schaefer pens handed down from father to son? No more. My wallet, which I used everyday for forty-six years, is setting a record. I bought it in Copenhagen, Denmark while stationed there during World War II. It was made to last. Hundreds of memories are in it. It's like a file of my complete life. We've had a long friendship. Nowadays, people have to buy a new one every year, so they miss out on many pleasant memories.

•

These new outside banking machines where you can get money twenty-four hours a day are for the birds. I have never used one and never will. In the first place, you should keep enough green stuff at home for emergencies. Secondly, using them after hours makes you a sitting duck for a robber or murderer. Thirdly, you already have a check book and a credit card that can get you money anywhere, anytime. And fourthly, who the hell wants to go to a machine when you can go inside and be greeted by a pretty teller who hands you your money and asks, "How is your lovely wife?"

•

In 1991, we had a terrible wind and rain storm in Phoenix, Arizona. Very unusual. In the morning there was untold debris everywhere in our apartment complex: fallen trees, branches, leaves, paper, miscellaneous debris, and dust in front of our doors, on walkways, sidewalks, and balconies. We got up and, first thing, got brooms, dustpans, and garbage cans to clean it up. I looked around and saw that the only ones cleaning up their apartment areas were over seventy: the Millers, the Hartmans, Francis Clark, Eileen Riordan, the Timmons, Georgie, and us. The kids in the complex came home from school and their parents came home at 5:00, and the junk was still there, hours later. I have to wonder: Is cleanliness only for the elderly and filth a badge of courage for the young?

•

It's a damn shame but if I hug a child, I can be accused of child molestation or pedophilia. If I hug a woman, I can be charged with sexual harassment, and if I hug another man, I can be suspected of being gay. I don't like to hug dogs, or cats, but if I did, I suppose I would have to get their permission. What a sick society we have become! Even a senior man, happily married for fifty-three years, can so easily be looked upon as a pervert.

•

Be nice to people you dislike. You can be nice by avoiding them. Remember, they probably don't like you either. So just think of the happiness you create when you don't see each other.

•

If you live long enough, you'll probably find yourself in the depths of boredom from time to time. As busy as I am, I get bored and I fight it by changing my routine to keep my daily life interesting. I goof it up ... do things in a different way ... do something that I don't usually do. It helps to keep life interesting and different, even after 80 years.

•

The "good old times" were really not that good. The good times are now, though we all have many problems — of identity, friendship, work, acceptability, spirituality, and commitment in a society whirling with crises. These times we live in will be great if we never lose faith — though there is no insurance policy. Life is a risk and you must commit yourself.

•

Death is an integral part of life. You know when you were born, but your death is not predated. What makes you think it will be ten years from now? What makes you think it won't be tonight? But if you knew you were going to die tonight, with what care would you love this day? How much more cheerful would you be? How much more understanding and kind would you be to your wife and children? How much more happiness would you create? How much more charity would you offer to the unfortunates? How much deeper would you look into the faces of your friends? Think it over — today — because death may come earlier than you think. Live each day as if it were your last. One day you will be right.

•

There is nothing more difficult for any of us than watching a dear one leave this earth. And nothing more sad than having them suffer. Yet, there is nothing more inspiring than to watch absolute peace triumph over illness. However, they never die — not those who led an exemplary life. We will continue, for years to come, to think and speak and write and talk about those who were blessed with wisdom, charity, compassion, kindness, honesty, perseverance, intelligence, and friendship. We will miss them, but we will never forget them.

People are afraid of change, but change is necessary. We cannot exist as if everything is poured in concrete. The upheavals of change give us the opportunity of learning more, maturing more, and finding unity with others and with life as a whole. Through experience of change, we become seasoned and gain a new and exciting overview of ourselves and our existence.

•

Every human should and will experience pain. Pain gives you compassion because it causes you to understand others.

•

All of us are composites of the good or bad people who influenced our lives. We are what we are because of the many people that we associated with: those we worked for and those we worked with, the people in religious cloth and the people in the marketplace, the poorest of the poor, to the richest of the rich. All of this affiliation provides an inestimable source of knowledge. What purpose is an education if all you learn is book knowledge? Everyone gets to be a Ph.D. when they apply what they learn through experience and application with others — be they peasant or president.

•

Each of us can work miracles. Just give a smile, a hand, or a kind word to someone. You don't have to feed the multitude or command wind or rain or change water to wine or make the blind see. Just give a touch of love and a smile of peace.

•

Truth is born through disagreements.

•

Courage is the first human quality because it is the quality that guarantees all others.

Remember, some changes may seem slow, like waiting for wind or water to erode a rock. But other changes happen rapidly, like watching a snow flake melt in the warmth of your hand.

•

With positive thoughts, kind words, an optimistic attitude, and unwavering faith, you can really make an important difference in yourself and others.

•

People don't laugh enough, I've always said. I realize that no one can laugh all the time — life with its problems and sickness, and death with its sadness does not permit it. Still, most of the time we can laugh. The mind and body are not separate entities. They are one, so bad emotions cause bodily illness. Whereas laughter heals all.

There is so much sadness in the world that I think the greatest gift we can give to one another is laughter. Laugh to remain sane — even at yourself. A sense of humor is vital to your health; without it life will be drab.

•

I don't know why but every time I write down the word diarrhea, I never spell it right and invariably have to look it up. You know: dyarea — diarhea — diahrea.

Health

A long life. You're 50-60-70-80 years old, and you want to live a longer, productive life? Easy! Just:Learn something new — if not every day, every third day. Exercise — every day; take a daily walk, not the car. Spend time with family and friends — every day! Eat healthy foods. Avoid excessive weight.

Have a good medical plan. If you don't use it, hooray and if you do, hooray. In either event, you'll have peace of mind. It's never too late to contribute. Grandma Moses painted at age 100. George Bernard Shaw wrote plays at 93. Albert Schweitzer ran

DFR Hospital at 89. Thomas Edison invented Dictaphone at 84. Ben Franklin helped write the constitution at 81. Colonel Sanders started Kentucky Fried Chicken (now KFC) at 66.

•

Operations. By age seventy-eight, I had fourteen operations, nine of a serious nature. I also had twelve days in critical isolated care with pneumonia in both lungs. And I'm still here. As I look back and reflect at all my incarcerations in hospitals, I remember this: no doctor ever sends you home well. He does what he can but, only what you do on your own when you get home will make you well again.

•

It is my obligation and duty in life not only to remain strong, but to continue to help the weak without becoming weak myself.

Faith

Soul Food. The only way you can feed your hunger is to go to a grocery store or an eating establishment. So the only way you can feed your soul is to go to church.

•

The role of any church has never been and should never be one of making you comfortable. It is the exact opposite. It should make you uncomfortable by forcing you to look around and see the deplorable misery that surrounds you and getting you to start thinking how you can improve it. Certainly we can treat less fortunate human beings with at least a small part of the attention and comfort that people lavish on their pets.

•

Dear God, You know I am really not a humble man. I have never been and never will be. If humility means what I think it does, to be modest or meek, lowly or unpretentious, how could I have ever risen above my origins? When I am striving for more and higher, I am sure, gracious God, you want me to excel. Now, God, since you have given me all these talents and abilities and taught me a sense of value, I've exhausted myself doing good. And I didn't get cocky or arrogant either. I think, however, I have a lot of pride — and God, I cannot believe that is one of the seven deadly sins. To me, pride is the pleasure of doing things well.

•

Don't keep the faith, spread it.

•

A church is not a cafeteria in which you take what you want and leave the rest.

•

Letter to a son. No clear-thinking adult can assume that life will be without problems and pain and disappointments. There are times when events go awry and you feel it as a personal tragedy. If your present hopes, whatever they are, don't come to fruition (and we pray that they do), so be it.

Generally, you'll realize that the problems of the moment are not your first disappointments. As you look back, you'll realize you may have made poor decisions, but you cannot agonize by saying, "I wish I hadda." You can't bring your moments of decision, which are dead, back to life.

Everyone suffers from many personal tragedies; we all get our share. That is the time to test your faith and go on to face another day, remembering, above all, how fortunate you have been in past successes. Post the Serenity Prayer over your mirror:

God grant me the serenity to accept the things I cannot change, the courage to change the things I can, and the wisdom to know the difference.

I pray every day to the Holy Spirit as my friend, to give me the light and the strength to do the right thing, not necessarily the most popular thing. And It has never failed to show me the way and to give me the strength of purpose to struggle on in the face of competition and adversity. As the years went by, I discovered that, when you decide to do something every day, come hell or high water, your life takes on a new purpose. You have the obligation to yourself to perform and you must not fail.

•

In church, we receive bodily communion with Christ in the shape of a wafer and wine. But equally important is the significance of all of us standing together in church, to testify to our love for each other. You miss this when you're "in the sack" or glued to the TV.

•

One of the greatest errors I can make is to have a dual moral standard, to profess my Catholic faith on one hand and violate the Church's rules on the other. If I claim to be a Catholic Christian, then I must not become a "Sunday Catholic" by attending church for one hour each week and then acting like a miserable human imbecile in the other 167 hours of the week.

I must strive to act morally always. I am human, so I can't possibly not violate some rules, sometime, somewhere. Nevertheless, I must get up, be sorry, and strive to be better. My church has always been countercultural; living in a secular world obeying religious principles is not easy. I must be aware of "forks in the road" of life — one way leading to my faith and the other to a life of violations of it.

Some things about my own Catholic church I believe are wrong or outdated. But we have to be patient and obey; it takes years for the hierarchy to decide what Pope John called "aggorniomento." Open the windows and let some fresh air in.

Faith is a divine faculty that comes from God as a gift. And you use it or you lose it. If you use it (and millions don't), you'll be amazed how it will shape your life positively. And it really works. Let your faith in your own abilities create success in anything you do. Let it be unyielding, steadfast, and never moved by negative thoughts. Rely on it, live by it. You can do it.

•

As a Catholic, I believe without proof, worship without reward, and pray without assurance.

Prayer

Everyone should pray, every day, and at night. It's the most remarkable therapy. It's a great bargain. It costs nothing. Through prayer, you can become a real somebody, without really trying. If you don't pray, you will lose your faith. When you lose your faith, you lose your love. When you lose your love, you lose yourself. And when you lose yourself, you have become worthless to everybody.

Family

The fourth commandment is "Honor thy father and mother." You would think, from the behavior of many people today that honoring parents really means just giving them a pleasant greeting when you see them. But it is deeper than that, and carries a lot more responsibility. It means:

1. Supporting them financially and physically. They carried you from ought to umpteen years — now it's your turn.

2. Respecting their rules, which are God's rules.

3. Never dishonoring the family name or causing them shame.

4. Defending them.

5. Never draining their finances because you drained yours.

6. Writing them, calling them, visiting them — with a gift, even a loaf of bread.

•

If children ignore guidance essential to the development of conscience and good character, they will never grow up or become wiser but instead remain self-centered, pleasure-driven, insecure, resentful, and irresponsible. (My parents, with second grade educations, taught us this.)

•

As a father replying to my son's questions, I had to work harder than a doctor dealing with life or death. The doctor is only responsible to his patient, but I am responsible to God!

•

Preface to my will: This will is not only a distribution of my earthly riches, but an endowment of my life's mature guidance to you. My endeavors to help the ill, deprived, needy, and uneducated by charitable activity was just as important as the desire for earthly possessions.

•

The Jesuits, a teaching religious order, used to have a saying, "Give me a child until the age of seven and you can have him the rest of your life." They knew full well that the character of all of us is shaped in the first seven years of childhood. Parents — remember this!

•

I read this somewhere. The Japanese see marriage as an investment, not as consumption. And they make it pay off rather than throwing it out when it gets old. And their children are a social investment so they're never left to chance. In America, 50 percent of all children will experience a family breakup before their 16th birthday, 25 percent will live with only one parent, and

20 percent will live in poverty. As an investment in society, the U.S. family has sadly experienced a decline in value during my lifetime.

•

I really believe that fathers and mothers who have caused the death of the family unit are creating all our social problems. Their children are not getting the guidance or discipline that sustains a family unit. Along with the lack of moral guides and values and the absence of spirituality, the destruction of the family unit is furthered by the welfare state, dislocations, separations, poor communications, and divorces. Children can find no purpose in life with such families and are led to hatred, destruction, violence, robbery, drugs, and sex. And these parent miscreants blame society and the government for the failure of their children. They expect a school teacher to baby-sit their children until school is over and then leave them to "do their own thing" until they're home. The children get bug-eyed watching TV as they gorge on junk food. When the parents come home, they throw some fast food on the coffee table while everyone watches TV. Good God, when do they study? Never! And then the next day they get up, bleary-eyed, and rush off to school for another baby-sitting session.

•

Poor children come from poor parents and dumb children come from dumb parents.

•

Subsidize your children or grandchildren with over-generous gifts, and you kill their incentive to labor and struggle to attain their goals by themselves. In every case, spoiling the young kills the will of the recipient to excel. If you bequeath them anything, it should be the work ethic to struggle on their own to fulfill their desires, so they can proudly say, "We did it on our own." Or they can wait around hoping you go soon enough for them to get the whole bundle without working.

•

If you want to live longer and happier, take daily notes on what you want to accomplish. You will have less frustration and anxiety caused by having forgotten something important. Remember. The faintest ink is more accurate than the strongest memory.

•

The family is supreme. It is omnipotent. Nothing else really matters. Your values must be home and hearth. Don't have your job take out so much time that you have to shortchange your children. One third of your week should be devoted to your family.

•

My children and grandchildren in Canada and America will be my best memorial, as their lives recollect and relive any good qualities I had.

•

I think the highest aspiration for me as a parent is to have my children and grandchildren, both American and Canadian, to develop common sense, not intellectually smug. I don't want their specialized competence and monetary success to blind them to religion, morals, and love of country, or for them to fail to instill these precious beliefs in their own children.

Time Savers

Change toilet paper before it runs out and use the little left for facial tissue. You would really look funny with your pants down, looking for another roll in the closet down the hall when company walks in unannounced.

Keep a set of basic tools — a hammer, pliers, files, screw drivers — in the kitchen drawer, under the bathroom sink, in your basement, your garage, and a small set in your car. If not, you waste valuable time running to the garage constantly.

Don't waste time going to the post office for a few stamps at a time. Buy $10 worth, keep them in a jar, and mail your letters in a nearby box.

Keep all staples, cups, writing supplies, etc., in small jars or boxes in one drawer — all at your fingertips.

Keep all repair tapes in one shoe box.

Keep bills, clippings, and communications that come into your home in boxes alphabetically. I witness so much waste of time by people looking for an address or a bill or a pamphlet. I claim you should be able to find any document you need in no more than twenty seconds. In a single year you will save two weeks — you can take a vacation!

My lovely wife is a classic example. When we were first married, I noticed her looking for fifteen minutes for an address. She kept addresses jammed in her purse with my old love letters, bills, old grocery tapes, keys to the house she sold years ago, used Kleenex, broken pencils, pens that died last year. Of course, she couldn't find the address. Good God, how? She has a lifetime of addresses scribbled on backs of envelopes, paper, parts of magazines, borders of Penney catalogs, and backs of old bills. She never did find the address, but she sifted through the refuse she dug out of her purse. She started to compare grocery prices from the old tapes and scowled at the inflated prices. But then, she started reading my old love letters. She smiled and sighed and blushed. You see. All was not lost!

Working

If you are looking for the best people in any organization, seek first enthusiasm. Without that, quit looking. Then look for intelligence, imagination, and creativity.

•   ◦

Quality is never an accident; it is always the result of high intention, sincere efforts, intelligent direction, and skillful execution. It represents wise choices from among many alternatives.

•

In business over forty years I wrote many ads. I had this card above my desk as a Penney adman and later as manager. I composed it, and it saved me lots of grief:

"Poor or hurried preparation by management causes poor, or hurried techniques by the ad artist, which causes poor sales results. If you have to hurry an ad, save your time and money. Throw the blank page into the waste basket before you start it."

•

Another warning I composed and had printed over my desk: "Every excellent ad you create will be the result of hard work and intense research — not happenstance. You will have to agonize and suffer somewhat over every one."

•

And as a Penney manager, I put this sign over my desk that superseded all: "It All Depends on You!"   Gentle readers — it really does!

•

Super achievers are motivated — not born to money and success.

•

It is much easier to prevent problems than to solve them under pressure.

•

If at first you don't succeed, try again — and again and again. Then quit! There's no sense in you making a damn fool of yourself.

Quality is never an accident; it is always the result of high intention, sincere efforts, intelligent direction, and skillful execution. It represents the wise choice of many alternatives.

Unions

I had a sister and five brothers and — financially and materially only —I excelled over all of them. They all were proud of my success and told everyone about it. Back in the Depression, I wasn't in a contest with my brothers, I just didn't want to work in the iron ore mines getting half-killed every day at low pay 1,400 feet underground. I could see that such work rewarded well only the English-speaking captains and management, not the workers, 90 percent of whom were displaced Europeans speaking no English.

I may sound like a union man, but nothing could be further from the truth. I never did and never would join a union. I did not want some union leader with less intelligence, honesty, and a lesser work ethic than I to decide how much, when, and how I was going to work and how much I would get paid. I wanted to advance on my own. Everyone should have that liberty.

TV

TV is the greatest family destroyer and the greatest destroyer of individuals. When you're watching TV:

You don't listen.
You don't read.
You don't talk.
You don't study.
You don't paint.
You don't write.

> You don't learn.
> You don't teach.
> You don't discuss.
> You don't question.
> You don't contribute anything.
> You don't communicate.
> You don't love.

As you can see, I am not a TV lover. Most programs are garbage. But I will walk ten miles to see another Archie Bunker show, a Lawrence Welk show, a Jacques Cousteau show, or the greatest movie ever — "Patton" (for the 9th time).

In 1950, when I was a young father in Crosby, Minnesota, everyone in town had a TV except us. My wife and I refused to succumb to the TV craze. Too poor? No, I was running the largest store (J.C. Penney's) in town and probably had the largest salary.

But one day my wife and I suddenly realized that we didn't see any of the kids in the neighborhood playing outdoors. They were all at home watching the "boob tube." And our sons were with them. So, we finally capitulated, in order to know where our kids were. However, my wife and I controlled the knob at specified "viewing times." After homework, the boys were allowed one hour of watching before dinner. After dinner, we made sure they studied some more before getting another possible hour of viewing. On Saturday mornings we allowed one hour of cartoons.

We kept to this schedule until they were fourteen years old, when they left home to attend St. John's Preparatory School, where they saw little TV. Their academic, sports, and religious schedules kept them busy from 5:00 a.m. to 9:00 p.m., which was severe but rewarding. How did these sons of ours turn out after being denied the many hours of TV viewing that present-day kids are allowed? They're both healthy, wealthy, and wise — and have never been a problem to us, are both smart, well-adjusted adults. Jeff runs his own advertising business. Mike is a doctor. He and his wife Annie have two great children, Aerie and Jess — outstanding students like their dad and uncle Jeff.

Mike raised his kids without a TV until they were around fourteen. He finally bought one in 1991 for the sole purpose of playing videotapes, so he could choose his own entertainment.

Television creates an insidious nether world over which you have no control. We may have a button to push to flick it all off, but we don't. We have become a nation of TV zombies.

I agree with Martha Griffiths, Lieutenant Governor of Michigan, who called the tube a monster. TV shows should have subtitles running across the bottom of the screen because the kids never see words. They get impressions of voices and situations and end up being unable to read or write.

Two out of three of our high school students don't know which century the Civil War in the U.S. was fought. One out of five believe the telephone was invented after 1950. In 1986, 700,000 kids graduated from high school and couldn't read their diplomas — twenty five percent of our teenagers dropped out of high school. One-fifth of all young working people read below the 8th grade level. American students ranked tenth in a 1985 assessment of math achievement; Japanese students ranked first. Meanwhile American kids watched an average of 15,000 hours of television between the ages of six to eighteen — 2,000 hours more than they spend in school!

Charity

You must remember, if you're going to raise money for any purpose, you had better be the first contributor with a generous check.

When answering prospective donors' questions about how much they should give, the best reply is "Give until you're proud."

•

There is no limit to the amount of good people can do if they don't care who gets the credit.

Friends

True friendship is a solid chain of giving and receiving.
I wrote this in calligraphy as a birthday message to my greatest Canadian friend, Frank Smith, on his 66th birthday:

"There are a few rare people who are as reliable as sunrise. You can see it in their smiles, feel it in their handshakes. You can tell that their lives are fulfilling, their work rewarding. Happiness is something they've created, not only for themselves but for everyone. They have the vision to do what is possible and the desire to do what is achievable. You can always rely on them to give their best every day. And you, Frankie, my dearest friend, are one — and I am the other.   Love, Joey"

Love

In 1984, my wife and I formed the greatest club in the world. It is the most exclusive organization anywhere because there are only two members — us!

•

Dear Friends: Sometime in the future one of you will die and leave the other to grieve and mourn. You may as well recognize the inevitable now. It's been eight months since my beloved wife Dorothy died and left me to cope with a long season of trial. I had no previous experience in enduring the sudden emptiness that ensued. However, my strong Catholic faith gave me sustenance, because I knew that He who took my wife and caused me this excruciating pain and sorrow, surely, in His goodness, would give me strength to endure them. And He did. So, prepare for your grieving now by having a loving, respectful relationship with your spouse so you will never have to apologize to anyone or to yourself if you are the survivor. Remember: God gave you a life and we all owe Him a death. Keep living in a full, happy, loving, and healthy relationship so the surviving spouse will draw from that love and find the strength to cope.

Dogs

Many people may be shocked to learn, after all these years, that I really don't love dogs but only tolerate them for the sake of my friends and relatives who do. People seem to have dogs to exact some love or obedience or admiration or devotion they can't get from human beings. All dogs do is eat, sleep, drink, and play, and their only contribution to society is to deposit urine or fecal matter on every lawn or tree in the area. If a dog-lover's children did this, all hell would break loose. Can you imagine the horror parents would feel on learning from a neighbor that their son had peed on their beautiful spruce or manicured lawn? Or that their daughter dropped her lace-edged panties and did the same? Not Bow Wow! but Pow Wow!

But the dog, after drenching the sofa or having diarrhea on the carpeting just wags his tail with forlorn eyes and is completely forgiven! And sometimes gets a kiss right on his drooling mouth. The tolerance and admiration and forgiveness people have for their dogs they would never have for any human beings.

I read somewhere that a couple of billion dollars every year are spent on dog food in the USA — twice as much as on baby food. Dog food accounts for eleven percent of supermarket sales of dry groceries. Seven and a half billion pounds of dog food are sold every year — that is more than the hamburger sold by McDonald's worldwide. And that's not all. Add the cost of the animals, breeders, veterinary care, medicines, vitamins, chewing bones, collars, bowls, leashes, sweaters, socks, sleep baskets, house cages, pillows, sleeping pads, dog beauty parlors, dog walkers, pooper scoopers, pooper pans, dog photographs, dog burials. Add it all up and Americans spend seven billion dollars a year on dogs. Seven billion! Ninety percent of the dogs in the U.S. eat and live better than 75 percent of the people in the world. Most of the dogs in America live and eat better than the children in the U.S. below the official poverty line. Seven billion dollars! Why? All they do for you owners is palpitate, pee and poop on your rugs, furniture, lawns, trees, and boulevards.

Of course, I would like to express my admiration for "seeing eye" dogs and "hearing aid" dogs and small dogs belonging to senior citizens and to the sick and physically impaired who enjoy their company. They do no harm and bring much comfort to the owners. And I love to watch hunting dogs.

Goose Story

In September of 1993 my wife and I were staying at our daughter's summer home on Lake Ontario. We went to mass at St. George the Great Catholic Church in Picton. They passed out their church bulletin after mass and my wife read it while returning to our daughter's home. She was really impressed with the article entitled "The Goose Story," and here it is verbatim:

"Next fall when you see geese heading south for the winter flying along in a "V" formation, you might be interested in knowing what science has discovered about why they fly that way. It has been learned that as each bird flaps its wings it creates an uplift for the bird immediately following. By flying in a "V" formation, the whole flock adds at least 71 percent greater flying range than if each bird flew on its own. Whenever a goose falls out of formation, it suddenly feels the drag and resistance of trying to do it alone so it quickly gets into formation to take advantage of the lifting power of the bird immediately in front. When the lead goose gets tired, he rotates back in the wing and another goose flies point. The geese honk from behind to encourage those up front to keep up their speed. Finally, when a goose gets sick or is wounded by gun shots and falls out, two geese fall out of formation and follow him down to help and protect him. They stay with him until he is able to fly or until he is dead. And then they launch out on their own or join another formation to catch up with their group."

And I say from the geese as humans, let's learn as a family and a community member —

1. To share a common sense of direction.
2. To stay in formation if we're going the same way.
3. To take turns at assisting each other.
4. To clap to encourage each other.
5. To stand by each other in distress.

The Author

Writing a book is a strenuous experience. A raconteur or story teller with an audience just lets the words flow out of his mouth as he entertains and enthuses those listening. He worries not one iota about spelling, sentence structure, dates, punctuation, or grammatical errors. And he gets the instant responses of his audience.

A writer does not have these advantages. He has to worry about all the above because he has a long line of critics. He himself is the worst, followed then by his wife, and then by the editor, copy editor, printer, and finally his readers — everyone trying to find fault, and rightfully so. And when it is done, there is no applause, no clapping of the hands — only silence. The writer and reader are hundreds and thousands of miles apart.

Favorite Philosophies

It's not so much who I am or who my ancestors were, but
what I can leave for others to enjoy and what my children can do
because of any spark I have ignited in them that really count.
— my brother Tony

ONE DAY, WAITING FOR MY CAR being repaired, I sat in a
dark, dim, oil-drenched room filled with auto parts old and new
next to the owner's "office" that was a dark, dim oil-drenched
room filled with mounds of paper, invoices, bills, and parts catalogs. And in this poorly lighted anteroom, I noticed an oil-
drenched sign on the wall which said, "I do my thing and you do
your thing. I am not in this world to live up to your expectations
and you are not in this world to live up to mine. You are you and I
am I. But if by chance we find each other, it'll be beautiful!"

•

My dear, dear friend Mona Winberg of Toronto who has
lived for sixty years as a victim of severe cerebral palsy struggled
this gem out of her paralyzed throat:

"When I go, I want the climate of heaven, but companions
from hell."

•

I have had many priests to whom I could turn to for sustenance and spiritual guidance. Two of them suggested the same
behavior. In 1954, Father Joseph Cashman in Crosby, Minnesota

and in 1984 Father Joseph Pranzo in Toronto — thirty years apart — offered the identical admonition:

"Serve best by example."

Isn't that something?

•

No one is entirely useless — even the worst of us can serve as bad examples.

•

Education consultant James Stension wrote:

"Children learn these inner strengths through word, example, and repeated practice. That is, they grow in moral strength from what they hear, from what they see and from what they are led repeatedly to do. They grow principally by imitating the strengths they witness in their parents or other adults whom they respect."

•

Too much emphasis on science and technology creates a danger of all peoples losing touch with those aspects of human knowledge and understanding that aspire to honesty and altruism. If materialism and technology are really the answers to all of humanity's problems, then the most advanced industrial societies would now be the happiest people on earth. But they are not! Equally, if people were meant to be only concerned with matters of faith and spirituality, then all would be living joyously according to their various beliefs — but they're not. Humanity can only fail to progress if we follow either course. We need both material and spiritual development or we are doomed to stagnate and die before our time.

— Dalai Lama

•

Faith and business or any profession or job properly blended can be a happy, wholesome, and even profitable mixture. God surely doesn't want you to work without profiting. A church-related religion should not be detached from life — something aloof and apart. Millions of businessmen and women have discovered the satisfaction of having God as a working partner. It puts integrity into their organization, sincerity into their sales, and monetary profits into their hearts and pockets.

— Billy Graham

•

From the book *Folklore of Canada* by Edith Fowke, on making maple sugar: "The older and stronger the trees, the better the sap and more abundant. A peculiarity which it would be well for each of us to be able to have said of his own life as it advanced."

•

I do the very best I know how. The very best I can, and I mean to keep doing so until the end. If the end brings me out all right, what is said against me won't amount to anything. If the end brings me out wrong, ten angels swearing I was right would make no difference.

— Abraham Lincoln

•

If I am not for myself, who will be for me? And if I am only for myself, what am I? And if not now, when?

— Hillel

•

Ninety percent of the world's ills are caused by poor communications.

•

Nothing is more frightening than ignorance in action.

— Goethe

Pleasure is the cessation of pain.
— Nietzche

•

Life doesn't guarantee that you will be liked by everyone. It's impossible. But there is an easy way to handle personal differences, courtesy of my great friend Helen Morrison. Because of her popularity, ingenuity, and good looks, I'm sure she had to ward off the barbs of jealousy. The plan is easy to remember. I have used it for forty-five years and, believe me, it works. It's called simply, ABC.

A. Avoid them
B . Black them out when you see them
C . Compassion — Pray for them

•

Seven commandments for an ideal life:
Intemperance - Greatest handicap you can burden yourself with
Concentration - Invaluable in any career
Introspection - Examine yourself
Body Care - Improves the mind
Money Making - Natural but if it's a sole objective it makes creatures poor at best
Punctuality - Easiest and rarest of virtues
Work - Open sesame to every door
— By Sir Frederic Williams-Taylor
General Manager of Bank of Montreal, Canada

•

If the primary aim of a captain were to preserve his ship he would keep it in port forever. The seas out there may be stormy, but conflict is the mother of creativity. If you take no risks, you will suffer no defeats, but if you take no risks you will win no victories.
— St. Thomas Aquinas

It is a sociological fact that people who are affiliated with or feel themselves a part of an organized religious structure and go to church regularly, do better in terms of all aspects of living. They cope better with problems, have stronger families, find and retain better employment, have more compassion for the poor and are a much happier lot.

— Linda Branki Cateura, Catholic USA Magazine

•

Sign in my church's sacristy in Phoenix: "Work for the Lord — the pay isn't very much, but the retirement is out of this world."

•

They lie and they even hate me because of my immense desire to succeed in my belief that endeavor thrives and merit advances where uniqueness of an individual is promoted and made much of and where success, not failure, is commended and admired.

— Margaret Thatcher, Prime Minister of England

•

In many ways the essence of a son's bond to his father is biological, organic, communal, mystic, and unsayable. It does not matter if one's father was a great capitalist or a bum, a scrap dealer or a con man, a millionaire or a drunk, or all of the above. A father sits like a squatter in his son's memory and never leaves. This is not because of pride or principle, but because of fate, love, resentment and gratitude. All which demands a reckoning, if not now, then later. The memory of one's father is a trick to beat back time — with the memory of his father's accomplishments.

— Ian Brown, Free Wheeling,
Canadian Tire family story

•

"Dovorey No Provorey" means "Trust, But Verify."
— Russian proverb

If you can trust a man, then a written contract is a waste of paper. And if you can't trust him, a written contract is still a waste of paper.

— J. Paul Getty, one of the world's
most successful businessmen

•

In 1948, Wallace Johnson, construction company owner (before he was to become a founding father of the world famous Holiday Inns) was fighting a re-zoning battle with the municipality of Memphis, Tennessee. He used the following text for his daily prayers: "Oh, Lord, make us one of the greatest leaders of the nation in the building of men and homes and help the City of Memphis to understand that this is our goal, so they will help us instead of hinder us. Oh, Lord, help me to be one of the biggest businessmen in the country, and if it be thy will, let me be a Vice-President of the National Home Builders Association. Amen." And he did it all!

•

In Phoenix, where we spend our winters, Father Henry Ferrera, aged seventy-four, retired as a Catholic priest after a fifty-year tenure of teaching biology, football and choir. Most of his football teams also had to sing in his choir. So those angelic young men in white choir robes later in the day would beat the hell out of each other on the football field. He spent a lifetime primarily helping poor youngsters. He said, "I told these poor kids that if anyone makes fun of you or tries to put you down, punch them out, and I'll swear on a stack of bibles that they ran into a door." He admitted that this philosophy often got him into trouble. And then he said, "You can't get to kids if all you do is preach to them."

The ultra rich families of Canada displayed little talent for the giving or taking of tenderness, greeting each other with dry pecks on the forehead where the gesture would be least likely to disturb makeup. Nobody ever genuinely hugged anybody. There was a strong suggestion even in their most intimate moments that they regarded love, like birth and death, as a quaint accident.

— Peter Newman, historian, in his book
on the rich families of Canada

•

You cannot shop around the rest of your life for beliefs that don't challenge your moral values.

•

Perseverance. "Nothing in the world can take the place of persistence. Persistence and determination are omnipotent."

— Calvin Coolidge, President of the U.S.

•

"The difference between a successful person and others is not a lack of knowledge but rather a lack of will."

— Vince Lombardi,
world's greatest football coach

•

Good judgment comes from experience and experience comes from poor judgment.

•

Do good to someone and that person will tell eight other people. Do bad and that person will tell sixteen.

•

The common denomination between true friends is not a common faith, but a genuine human compassion and loyalty which survives when all else fails.

— from the book *Job: the 1st Dissident,*
by William Safire

•

An expert is just an ordinary guy away from home.

Communism —- (Canadian dictionary) — a social system char-
acterized by the absence of classes and by common ownership of
the means of production and sustenance.
Communism — (USA dictionary) — government control of
goods and services as a social system supplying the necessary pro-
visions for labor and distribution.

•

Yul Brynner wrote:

Doomsayers tell you that, no matter how good you are,
your chances of achieving recognition are practically nonexistent.
And that even if you are the one in a thousand that beats the odds,
you will be facing a flock of indifferent and disappointing years.
Well, these perpetual Cassandras may be right — up to a point!

Yes, the going will be tough, especially if you're a doom-
sayer. However, if it isn't, I suggest you start worrying. Yes, there
will be difficult and disappointing years, especially if you're a
weakling. But I'll wager that you won't want to ever forget them.
Meanwhile I give you the Brynner plan for making your path to
success a little less painful.

First off, begin with creating individuality. What do I mean
by that? If you ask five artists to paint the same scene, I feel certain that all five paintings won't be exactly alike. They are not
cameras. Neither should you be. The chief curse of modern
mankind is uniformity. That's so wrong. Each one of us should be
known for possessing something unique. If you're not going to be
criticized because of that peculiarity, I recommend that you go
public with it. So what if you're called whimsical, dreamer, odd-
ball, or even kooky — at least you'll be called!

Give more consideration to your body. Make it your best
line of defense, as well as offense. Train it to express joy, sorrow,
pity, anxiety, honesty, et cetera, et cetera. This can be done by
enlarging the circle of your interests. Study those you believe excel

in these areas, cultivate them as friends.

Concentrate on the leaders — study their reactions, their points of view, their concepts, their opinions. Try to find out why they feel this way, but don't allow them to over awe you. Under no circumstances should you grant them that privilege. I've found that the moment you allow someone to feel he's superior, you are in for serious setbacks. After all, Hamlet was just another guy.

The next step is to develop your imagination. As of now it is probably limited to your past and present. Things that you did or are doing. Undoubtedly, you have daydreams, but, if you're like most people, you decide they are just that — daydreams! Well, start pretending, start thinking about the future, start exciting your ego. I'm not suggesting that you begin living a life of make-believe, but why not try just a little of it? Look more intently into your own image. Remember that success is not immoral.

•

Character is described as the deeper level of will and motive, of values and beliefs. A strong moral sense of right and wrong is inculcated into us and deeply embedded in us by our concerned parents who hold fast to certain basic moral principles that tell us right from wrong. Good character is formed in large part at an early age. It is neither inherent nor reflexive (having respect for something in the past). It must be cultivated at an early age by concerned parents who afford moral guidance from infancy onward.

— from the book *Question of Character, the Life of
John F. Kennedy* by Thomas C. Reeves

•

It's not so much who I am or who my ancestors were, but what I can leave for others to enjoy and what my children can do because of any spark I have ignited in them that really count.

— my brother Tony

Miss Me — But Let Me Go

When I come to the end of the road
and the sun has set for me
I want no rites in a gloom filled room;
Why cry for a soul set free?

Miss me — but not too long
And not with your head bowed low;
Remember the love that we once shared
Miss me — but Let Me Go!

For this a journey we all must take
and each must go alone;
It's all part of the Master's plan
A step on the road to home.

When you are lonely and sick of heart
Go to the friends we know
And bury your sorrows doing good deeds
Miss me — but Let Me Go!

Will You and I Be One?

Dear reader — will you and I be one?

Death is nothing at all. I have only slipped away into the next room. I am I and you are you. Whatever we were to each other, that we still are. Call me by my old familiar name, speak to me in the easy way that you always used. Put no difference into your tone, wear no air of forced solemnity or sorrow, laugh as we always laughed — at the jokes we enjoyed together. Play, smile, think of me, pray for me, let my name be the household word that it always was. Let it be spoken without effort, without the ghost of a shadow in it. Life means all that it ever meant. It is the same as it ever was. There is absolute unbroken continuity. What is death, but a negligible accident? Why should I be out of your mind because I am out of your sight? All is well. Nothing is past. Nothing is lost. One brief moment and all will be well as it was before.

—Author unknown

•

Fifty years ago I read this somewhere and, unbelievably, it popped in my mind today, and I remembered every word. It really gets you thinking. It says:

"A woman smiles, entrances, beguiles. Mere man succumbs to feminine wiles. Events transpire, suppressed desire sears the soul with consuming fire. With the dawn he is gone, but woman glorious every victorious slumbers on. Would I could see, it bewilders me: Who is the conquered — he or she?"

•

Irving Thalberg, at age twenty-one, the greatest Hollywood producer, died tragically at thirty-seven. This was his credo: "Never take any one man's opinion as final. Never take your own opinion as final, and never expect anyone to help you but yourself."

•

I had this on my desk for more than forty years. Abraham Lincoln's "Ten Cannots":
You cannot bring about prosperity by discouraging thrift.
You cannot strengthen the weak by weakening the strong.
You cannot help small men by tearing down big men.
You cannot help the poor by destroying the rich.
You cannot lift the wage earner by pulling down the wage payer.
You cannot keep out of trouble by spending more than your income.

You cannot further brotherhood of men by inciting class hatred.
You cannot establish sound security on borrowed money.
You cannot build character and courage by taking away a man's initiative.
You cannot really help men by having the government tax them to do for them what they can and should do for themselves.

•

Life is not easy and it is not going to be easy, and least of all, is it easy for either men or nation that spires to do great deeds. If you want ease, make up your mind that when you come to the end of your life, as you look back you will remember only ignoble things. If ease is what you want, and it is the first desideratum of your life, you can count but little in any way in your family, in your church, in your occupation or in your nation as a force in the social organization at large. And what is true of the individual is true of the nation.

— Theodore Roosevelt, President U.S.

•

In his book *Snake*, Ken "Snake" Stabler, one of the greatest football quarterbacks in history said the following about retirement. I believe Ken and I have something in common!

"I decided to take time in pursuing my future career, but I hope I'll be able to do something that will satisfy my ego, my ambition, and my need for recognition the way football did. I know I'm ambitious and that I have so much nervous energy I seldom can relax. I've always felt that I had to keep striving to get all I could out of myself in whatever I did. That life is a never ending struggle to keep pushing to do better to achieve and keep achieving. I have never yet achieved total contentment because I've never fulfilled all my ambitions, and I never will. There will always be something else to go after. The only semblance of content for me has been in the striving. People who keep pushing and pushing don't necessarily die earlier. Not if they take care of themselves. You have to keep going because if you accept the end, you lose. For a competitive sonofabitch like me, there can't be any limit, any end in sight. When you've done something successful for a long period of time, some people might not think they can do something else as well. I think I can, I have to find out one way or the other."

•

To laugh often and much. To win the respect of intelligent people and the affection of children. To earn the appreciation of honest critics and to endure the betrayal of false friends. To appreciate beauty and to find the best in others. To leave the world a bit better by a healthy child, a garden patch, or a redeemed social condition. To know even one life has breathed easier because you have lived. This is to have succeeded.

— adapted from B. Stanley

•

You are never old — old age is always fifteen years older than you are now.

•

The 6 most important words: "I admit I made a mistake."
The 5 most important words: "You did a great job."
The 4 most important words: "What is your opinion?"
The 3 most important words: "I love you."
The 2 most important words: "Thank you."
The least important word: "I."

— Anonymous